A D A M

I cannot help but sit here. I am not the least bit attracted to
this immobility. There is no necessity. I am not resentful.
What rational being would be resentful.

There is upward and downward. I am vaguely comfortable
here in old age.

Simple enough. I lie down more than a great deal. I sleep.
Slowly easing my way out of wakefulness. I sleep fourteen,
eighteen hours a day. But what is this sleep? I can be sure it
isn't a mystical position, I do not believe in psychoanalysis.
My sleep is merely my sleep, which I enjoy.

I used to sleep and remember. I was disappearing from
living. Dissolving. Foam. I don't think I was awake more than
one hour a day. Mind drifting in an abstraction of phantom
images. A blur of half formed words and images, and my
eyes would close. I would watch myself walking into an old
building, up a flight of stairs, entering a room: living the life
that I have lived, living the soft images. And I would wake

seated at a table talking to the boy about the most important events of the day. Which day? That was the problem. Which day was I a part of?

Not much of any day. These were to be my last moments before my complete disappearance from any semblance of living. Not physical pain but the absence of any presence. Not dread. Not despair. The mind became haze.

But then, waking. I was not alone. At first I thought it was still sleep, a dream, a past, an illusion. But he spoke directly to me. He was sitting in a chair next to me. Waiting while I slept. Watching. Studying my form.

I watched him for a while.

His face was immobile while waiting for my response to a question. But I didn't remember any question. He was too clear an image. He didn't represent anything. An unusual presence in my environment.

In all probability I closed my eyes.

"Excuse me," he might have said.

"Excuse me," he might have said again.

I could have opened my eyes at this point or merely have drifted further away. But certainly at one point this day or one day in the following weeks, contact was made.

◆◆◆

He is very young, a child, ten to twelve years old. At the age of obedience. He has long curly brown hair. A facial expression dominated by eyes that even in sternness have a curious vitality as though on the edge of a moment of humour.

The tray he carries is my meal for the day. He sets it on the small table on the far side of the room, in a section which is not my bedroom or my workroom. Arranges the plates and cutlery. Pours the water from the pitcher to the glass. Spreads the serviette and places the knife and fork to the left and the spoon to the right. Pulls up a chair and waits for me. He knows that I have been studying him, silently.

He enjoys watching me eat. Sometimes we talk. Not today. Since he has nothing to say, I have no enticement spurring me to speech. When I am done, he collects the scraps and the accoutrements from the table and places them on his tray.

He exits, saying, "Good evening sir." The small formality makes both of us appear important.

♦♦♦

"One cannot simply adopt correct positions and wait to be proven right."

The air was heavy, threatening rain. We sat in the smoky cafe. A large truck stalled outside the window and two men in blue coveralls were arguing over the engine, waving wrenches at each other, passing them over the steaming metal of a still engine. They reminded me of Indian shamans chanting, waving talismans over a sick body. But this body was metal and the time was not prehistory but the early twentieth century.

"You could wait for the historical process to provide the circumstances."

"Sure," I laughed at Mussolini's bait, "wait for all the wheels on the cart to be lined up perfectly, the slope of the grade slightly declined, the horse tethered and fed, before even imagining the raising of the whip and..."

"That's just the point...everything is in place, yet it remains necessary to raise and crack the whip on the horse's back before there can be any real motion.

"The circumstances always exist to topple the ruling class if the true revolutionaries are recognized by the masses."

"Mussolini, how can you expect us to recognize the true revolutionaries? Can we tell one whip from another?"

"But we don't use a whip. We use support, acknowledgement."

The truck was now billowing smoke, threatening to explode. One workman had abandoned his position on the running board while the other was standing in the smoke staring at the engine, his right hand raised, clutching a large wrench. The first few drops of rain were hitting the hot metal and steaming.

"It is only through the broad support of the masses that socialism will be ushered in, not through historical circumstances and theory alone."

"But not devoid of either."

The wrench descended, found a nut and with a dry groan, turned. The engine coughed and turned over, running perfectly.

"Is it incorrect to imagine that the masses will join when

the situation is ripe and the crest of the revolutionary wave is at its highest point?"

The waiter brought us the bill. "Only by cultivating the masses' support now can it spontaneously be called upon at the appropriate moment."

◆◆◆

There is a persistent knocking at the door, my door. No voice, but this loud flesh against wood demanding my response.

I refuse to move from the bed.

The sounds make me suspect the night has ended and the day begun, but the total absence of light in my room is proof that the night continues.

The knocking stops for an instant and then resumes.

There is no need to pull the covers over my head or bury my ears in the pillow. There have always been voices outside the room making persistent demands, passing orders. The knocking wants a voice to return its ugly demands. But I am safe in my relaxed silence, content that they are still concerned enough about my presence to wait at my door. But I will not announce them.

◆◆◆

If I open my door the boy will rush in to pester me with questions. Did you really live in Italy during the war? Did you kill anyone? What did he look like dead? And I will be forced to return once more to the events. The intense desperation and contempt in the tyrant's eyes as I lowered the gun. The dry, hollow click of metal against metal as I pulled the trigger and the gun jammed.

Is this what the intruder wants described here in my small room? Does he understand that he wants to be taken out of the present day, out of this cold city Toronto into the mountains of Como, into a day which continues to exist in this room only, at this table, as an old man slowly eats his lunch and a young boy devours the past?

◆◆◆

"Do you think it is the individual they detest while loving humanity, or is it humanity they detest while loving the individual?" Mussolini always laughed at his own jokes

Our first years in Turin were formidable. As the editor of *Avanti* and with his great power as a public speaker, Mussolini was the acknowledged leader of the party's left wing.

Turin was the centre. We sat in cafes, drinking, talking through the night about its history, its potential. The proletariat of Turin were the most advanced and combative in Italy. As early as 1904 we demonstrated a high degree of solidarity, and a readiness to take to the streets. We cluttered the table with empty bottles, discussing the massive defeats suffered in 1907 and, with the hindsight of idealistic theorists, how these could have been avoided. Without a doubt the 1912 metalworkers' strike "to the end" filled us with the greatest reverence. No difference that after seventy-five days of struggle they were said to be defeated — no more difference than the collapse of the FIOM in 1913 after their ninety-three days.

From these struggles considerable victories were acquired. We knew from the numerous examples of the Turin workers that we were the real enemy of the Northern industrialists and the potential ally of the peasant masses of the South.

His influence was great. We could find fault with his ideas and actions but seldom with Mussolini himself. A blind spot. We laughed with delight at his bombastic speeches against the passivity of the reformist party officials. And who could not but admire his charged writing exalting the combativity of the masses and the potentialities of the general strike as a weapon in the class war. Our admiration and loyalty were cemented by Mussolini's passionate opposition to all forms of militarism.

◆◆◆

Some days this boy devastates my ability to remember. His eager presence waiting for my recollection forces me to think only of his waiting. His impatience to ask me questions erases all answers. If he would sit quietly in a far corner of the room I might release the complete story, describe in empathy inspiring detail my inner feelings during the event. But his expectations are a constricting demand on the possibility of articulation.

The nervous manner in which this boy leans forward in the chair, the constantly half-open mouth, the shaking legs. He is safer outside the door.

Possibly if I talk in a whisper to the closed door it will be enough to satisfy this boy's hungry ears, to satisfy his morbid longing for the details of death.

He demands from me the articulation of an absent history, one of life's mysteries. But I refuse and will continue to do so as long as he waits. My patience is greater than the curiosity of his youth.

Discomfort grows as he sits on the bare wood floor, staring down the walls of the corridor at the door of his expectations. It is at the end of this narrow hallway, behind the closed gray door, in my room, on a vinyl-covered bent chrome chair that I sit feeling the energy of his curiosity.

◆◆◆

Out of idealism and necessity I was employed at the Fiat factory in Turin. I laboured in a physically difficult and low-paying position in the ball-bearing section of the plant.

The unbearable noise of the machines, the echos, the constant screechings which accumulate and push against your ears, entering your brain with such unrestrainable force that after a very short time you become one with the noise, you become a sound, just one more entity in a metal whole. It is similar to entering cold water, slowly, the cold repelling, but once immersed the blood and skin adapt, take on the characteristics of the sea and you change from a swimmer fighting the water into a part of the water, a wave moving with other waves. It's not that you no longer hear the noise; you are the noise. You have no other choice. It is the only possible escape.

The heat. At the beginning, in the early morning the machines are cold, almost cadaverous. The first whistle, the switches are thrown and they come slowly to life, the heat beginning to emanate. At first it is welcome against the chill of the morning and the men brush themselves against the warm metal, rubbing their thighs against the legs of the machine. Within the first hour shirts are removed and sweat is flowing freely from every body in the large room. By noon the machines are hostile, if a hand touches them it is instantly seared and, despite the unbearable heat, thick gloves must be worn constantly. A thick cloud of steam encloses the room, bodies emerge from and disappear into the haze — an arm, disemboweled, reaches out and deposits a ball bearing into a tray and then suddenly disappears, ingested by the machine.

Mussolini has finished his coffee and is looking for the waiter. He is able to listen. Although its difficult, you may describe the taste of a particular food to some one who has never experienced it, relating the aroma, the texture, comparing it to foods which are similar. But pain eludes the mechanics of description. Mussolini may empathize, but he cannot feel the machines.

Our friendship is becoming strained — he becomes more anaemic, taking his pallor from the paper of his writing and editing, as I become blacker and blacker with layers of dirt and grease from the machines.

◆◆◆

Today is anger. Dislike. The top of my head is a discomfort which I attempt to pass on to whoever comes within my proximity. The young boy who brings my food is not amused by the insults leveled at the over cooked roast beef. There is no blood left in this meat, it looks and tastes like old leather. He couldn't care less if the meat is too rare or too well done. This child thinks he has more important concerns to occupy his waking hours. But still he waits to hear my story.

It came as a shock to realize I could kill him. I felt the inevitability of my decision. I'm going to kill him. I must. Mussolini betrayed our cause. The hypocrisy of the man, preaching socialism, equality of the people. Writing accusatory articles. Publishing his socialist newspaper. He was nothing more than a dandy. Prancing the street. Shouting slogans. I believed him. Helped him when he was arrested. I'll kill him. If only I knew where he is hidden. It couldn't be far from here. He sits silent without apology across the narrow table. There are rumours. The people talk to us. They hate the tyrant almost as much as we do. Everyone is an anti-fascist now, almost enough to make you believe there never was such a thing as fascism three weeks ago. They have literally vanished into thin air. But where were the anti-fascists when there were just a few of us fighting in the darkness. I'll take their information and food but I want the pleasure for myself of aiming the gun, of watching the butcher squirm, begging for his pitiful life, of pulling the trigger, of watching his diseased blood spill, of hearing his last pathetic breath and gasp of life.

The nights are cold but this meat is horrible. How dare you betray me with this slop.

And the tramp, his mistress, I hear she is with him. For all I care, she can live.

It's this meat, it must be rancid. Are you trying to poison me? How can I let him live?

♦♦♦

We called it Mussolini's defection. In 1914 Mussolini became an advocate of Italian intervention into the war. The official party position was defined as: "Neither support nor sabotage." The party leadership remained true to its "abstentionist" principles.

♦♦♦

Sometimes I suddenly stop talking. Look at the boy. I say nothing, I just stare at a point, at something, at someone behind him. But nothing is there, no one is there. And the longer I don't say anything the more the boy's mouth opens, quivers, about to speak. He listens more attentively. Maybe I'm whispering. "Excuse me. I beg your pardon." But I refuse to answer.

◆◆◆

I seldom look out the window. My table is situated facing a wall. To look out the window demands the effort of turning 180 degrees in my chair. The view is seldom worth the necessary expenditure of energy.

If I looked out the window I would see a black cat sitting in a patch of slightly moist grass staring at a large black bird. The cat is not sure whether to attack or to retreat from this giant crow. The bird is nonplussed. Darkness has already begun. The cat slowly creeps closer. The crow stretches its wings. A black mass swoops. The cat has only darkness in which to hide, pressing itself into the ground, waiting for the claws and talons of death. The cat guessed wrong. The relationship of predator and victim is a volatile affair, sudden reverses of position should not be unexpected.

◆◆◆

I have only one truly sophisticated desire and function in life, to sleep. Here, despite all the extraneous divergences of active life, is where I excel. Sleep is my speciality.

My hope is that I will die in bed; the most perfect of immobilities, the most proper function for a bed. A pillow and the drifting from a dream into the thickest black would be my choice. But when is the last time I had a choice?

He waits for my eyes to open, for my words to pronounce presence. He studies me if I am awake or asleep. I prefer sleep to all other states, it is only here I come close to my true self.

So why is it that my wakefulness has so quickly become a habit?

◆◆◆

A hand rudely shaking my shoulder, "Walter, Walter." The foreman, I had fallen asleep at my machine, but no, it wasn't a boot it was a weak hand.

"Mussolini, is it serious? has the army...?"

"No nothing serious. I have just finished an article. You must read it, shall I read it to you?"

He was leaning over my bed, waving a thin flag of handwritten pages. Wild drunken eyes demanding my attention.

"It is my new political initiative."

"I'd rather sleep." The oppressive thought: in a few quick hours I would be standing beside the machine, standing and bending for eleven or twelve hours.

"A cup of coffee."

I sat on the bed's edge, slowly drank, yawned, he read. From what I can remember, it was a brilliant paper, in essence a defense of Mussolini's position of shifting away from the official party position of neutrality in the war. He appeared to be motivated by scorn for the passivity of the official party position toward the war of "neither support, nor sabotage," describing it as a policy of "clean hands."

There was one section which particularly struck me:

"Revolutionaries see history as a creation of their own spirit" — how many times had we discussed this very notion — "as being made up of a continuous series of violent tugs at the other forces of society — both active and passive, and they prepare the maximum of favourable conditions for the definitive tug (revolution); they must not be content with the provisional slogan 'absolute neutrality,' but must transform it into that of 'active, operative neutrality.'"

Finished reading I found him staring at me intently, waiting for a response, an expectant child, uncertain of the consequences of an action — would it be a punishment or a reward.

"Brilliant."

A smile spread across his face.

"But..."

A frown began to appear. "But what, but... "

"But, are you sure? Your position might be easily misconstrued, bent to fix on the notion of 'active' as opposed to 'neutral'."

"Of course, of course that would be a misinterpretation. I am not opposed to neutrality, but rather opposed to the notion of an inactive instead of an active neutrality."

"No, I mean, I agree with you, the party is trying to fix us in a position of nonaction, but will it be possible to carry on an active neutrality without loosing the position of neutrality itself, and becoming involved militarily?"

"No, it is just that we no longer can endure the bloodless, clean-hands policy of the party."

The remaining few hours before work we spent in coffee and loud debate. Mussolini was like a parent with a newborn child, it could defaecate all over him but do no wrong.

But within weeks the true meaning of Mussolini's text became clear. The "active, operative neutrality" was actually one of intervention into the war. Any notions of neutrality were to be forgotten. The bloodless party policy had to be infused with action and blood.

This was Mussolini's first bite. I had suspected there was a snarl hidden behind the dog's smile, but who at the time could have envisioned the extent of his ability to lie?

◆◆◆

Some days it takes all my effort to remember the details of the event. If I didn't know better, I would doubt anything actually occurred. These are the days of defence, the days of block, the days when the head is composed of incoherent thoughts, the irritating spin of dislocated memory, the whirlwind of translucent images. These are the rare days. On most, it is the clear image of the gun and Mussolini's face. Claretta Petacci's expression is always frozen in a frightened scream.

◆◆◆

My gun continues to jam. What could be more frustrating than to point a gun against a tyrant, to pull the trigger and be answered with only silence? The dull thud of the failed gun. To confront a man with his death, to instill the final fear deserves the courtesy of completion. It is an action once instigated which demands completion.

◆◆◆

The jamming of the second gun was impossible. That one would not work was a shock, but not out of the ordinary. When the second gun also refused to respond, was it a sign? An outside force was intervening in the execution? The tyrant had to die. Could it be possible that I was not to be the messenger of justice? Was it written that someone else would administer the verdict?

Mussolini's face after the second gun refused to work was set in anger not fear. What a fool of an executioner. But the third gun.

♦♦♦

The effect of my employment could be directly measured in my desire to explode the system from within and from without — my ardent socialism calcified and a belief in the necessity of temporary anarchism developed. Mussolini and I drifted apart.

When the news of the February Revolution in Russia was beginning to filter through to us in Turin, I met Mussolini in a small cafe seated with a number of his newspaper friends discussing the events and attempting to judge their significance. The censored press reports were sketchy and I was hungry for any information. When I joined them the heated discussion diminished only slightly for polite introductions.

"The bourgeois press has told us how the autocracy's power has been replaced by another power which is not yet clearly defined and which they hope is bourgeois power."

The waiter, a fat bald man, stood beside the table listening, his face contorting with the conversation, a face which appeared to be collapsing in on itself.

"They have been quick to establish a parallel between the Russian Revolution and the French Revolution, and have found that the wants are similar."

"I'm not convinced that the Russian Revolution may not be simply an event, but a proletarian act."

To the waiter it didn't matter who held power, the proletariat or the aristocracy, as long as both drank and tipped, so his display of grimaces was not demonstrating approval or disapproval, but some other meaning.

"Therefore, I presume you expect it will debauch into a socialist regime."

"The Bolsheviks are not Marxists."

"They live the thought of Marx, that which can never die, which is the contamination of Italian and German idealist thought."

What was wrong with the waiter's mouth? It was as though he had unexpectedly eaten a hot pepper and was suddenly feeling its effects and simultaneously trying to hide it from anyone who might be watching. Could it be possible that the Russian Revolution was of paramount importance to this effeminate waiter, and what I was watching was his unsuccessful attempt to hide his overwrought excitement?

"I reject the Marxist notion that there is a fatal necessity for a bourgeoisie to be formed in Russia, before the proletariat might even think of rising up, for their own class demands, for their own revolution."

I shouted out in my anger. Pounded my fist against the table, knocking over two half-empty glasses. "It's not an idea, it's not an intellectual chess game, it's already occurring. And here in Turin we have to do the same, we must act now and follow the Russian example."

They stared at me, politely sipped their aperitifs, nodded as you would at any madman or animal out of control and slowly returned to their pros and cons, their careful weighing of the possibilities of the situation.

The waiter wiped the spilt liquor off the table and resumed his position beside the table ready to contort his face further in rhythm with the conversation.

I left the cafe seething, walked the streets for hours wondering how our intellectual leaders could be so blind to the situation. The impact of the Russian Revolution of 1917 was perhaps more rapid in Turin than anywhere else in Europe. Hostility to the war had been general in the city from the start, and had grown in intensity as the conflict continued. The first months of 1917 were punctuated by numerous industrial struggles launched to counter the effects of food shortages and rising prices.

What did these cafe intellectuals know of the women workers in the textile factories and their position at the vanguard of the struggle? Had they been at any of the meetings where the workers had been told to return to future meetings with revolvers? Did they know it was imperative to waste no time, to work actively for a general insurrection, to get hold of bombs? Did they know what was seizing the imagination of the mass of workers in the other Italian cities? They spent their days in their newspaper offices, not in the violence of the factories.

And in the heat of the summer in August 1917, on the occasion of yet another failure of bread supplies, it did come, the rising of the Turin proletariat in a spontaneous insurrection. We built barricades in the working-class quarters. The centre of the city was besieged. The day of our revolution had come, guns and bombs had been brought out. But by whose orders, under whose command? Our command. It was spontaneous. As far as there was any organization it was provided by the anarchists.

The socialist leaders, the trade union officials, where were they? Asleep in their beds, imposters, useless, voiceless. When we raised our guns against the tanks and machine-guns of the government troops how useless the theorists' papers seemed. How useless were their thin words against the onslaught of bullets and shells. For four days we fought. Women and men together, from our windows, from our barricades throwing crudely made bombs at the tanks as they turned their turrets and blasted our homes, our furniture, our hopes. When the last barricade fell there were over fifty workers lying dead. A thousand were subsequently either imprisoned or sent to the front by order of the courts. We lost this battle but we had demonstrated with an unequivocable rhetoric of action the immense revolutionary spirit of the Turin workers and without any doubt the impotent, wretched inadequacy of the socialist political organizations.

◆◆◆

The first bullets were for the screaming Claretta who insisted hysterically on throwing her arms around Mussolini's neck. We always intended that she too would die, but not first.

Only after suffering the death of her lover.

◆◆◆

It's not that I have not been accepted, not that one locale hasn't opened itself to receive me. It's rather, I've not found one specific point from where I want to continue. This room, why this particular room? Is it the specifics of this room in Toronto which compels me to be here? The green vinyl floor, the green bedspread, the brown table lamp with its cloth fringes, the overhead fixture with its plastic crystal baubles unsuccessfully attempting a chandelier, the small brown arborite table, it couldn't be these particular furnishings holding me here? It couldn't be the yellowed floral wallpaper. No, not the eternal trappings of my room which engage me. Not the present. I am hardly here. But the boy, Adam. Another force which provides me the energy to continue. This demand to move tugging at my body. This 'continue' toys with my patience. This necessity not to rest. Constantly nervous? What has happened to my sleep?

◆◆◆

A black grain blown freely by the wind.

✦✦✦

The war was finally over. The one thing we all believed, the workers, the socialists, the rulers, was in the inevitability of the revolution. It was merely a matter of when. For two years it was always just a matter of time. Always waiting. Organizing for the moment of the great revolution.

Big capital had been shocked by our growth, revolted by the gains made by the workers and the socialists during the two years which promised the birth of our revolution. They desperately searched for some instrument that could crush the soft skull of the child before it was able to take its first true steps. The employers would not be satisfied with any compromise to their powerful position.

In the autumn of 1920 the fascist squads began their raids. The landowners of North and Central Italy had found their cuddle. Mussolini stretched out his open hands and they were gladly filled by the industrialists. Mussolini's club came down against the socialist peasant associations, against socialist controlled municipalities, against socialist papers with such brutal force and accuracy that by 1921 the revolution was dead. No hope was left for a revolutionary vanguard party to lead an assault on the bourgeois State, the revolutionary potential had been murdered in its sleep. A monster had been released from its pit, paid by greedy capitalist fears to rise up and kill.

Its first tastes of blood and victory were intoxicating. The masters having destroyed the socialist threat would have returned the killer to the darkness, but their misfortunes were only beginning; by their own hand they had created the seeds of their own destruction. Mussolini having turned traitor to socialism, having become the murderer of the revolution was now looking for fresh bodies on which to exercise his well-sharpened teeth.

✦✦✦

There are individuals who live each day in pain. A constant gnawing at the body; a sharp series of jabs to the brain every few seconds; the jolt of a screaming stab from somewhere in the chest. If pain is registered long enough from a specific locale the body will memorize the pain, even if the ailment is alleviated, the pain persists.

This pain is not merely the itching of a phantom limb, but the sharp helplessness of a punch to the groin. So each day I do not feel terrible, I think myself fortunate.

THE MACHINE

He is knocking at the door. How arrogant. When he was
five years younger he wouldn't have dared. The audacity.
Soon he will be entering without permission. He wants to
hear more and more. The fascination has become an
obsession; I thought as he grew older his demands would be
satiated by the one incident, the pure moment. Merely a
moment.

But now he wants to know more than an historical detail.
He wants to know history. He has arrived at the stained door
of politics.

When he used to wait down the hall, he was indulging in
the mystery of a particular; he was a mere boy. As a young
man it is not enough to know about the day, or the preceding
few events. Now he is scratching about in the epoch, trying to
absorb a cross-section of history. At this rate, in a month he
will be after my cultural history. He asks the most difficult
questions.

"What is it that made Mussolini change from a socialist to a fascist?"

He has brought me lunch. I certainly hope it is better than yesterday's.

"What motivated the man?"

Here it is, politics. The true meaning of the word.

What exactly did it mean that Mussolini's father was a passionate socialist? His first born Benito Amilcare Andrea; after Benito Juarez the native Mexican revolutionary who led the revolt and dispossession of the puppet Emperor Maximilian; after Amilcare Cipriani, an anarchist of their province; and after Andrea Costa, one of the founders of the Italian Socialist Party.

The proud father would spend hours by the crib reading political works to the infant Mussolini. A blacksmith who spent most of his time with his mistress, shouting his political opinions at the local bar.

His mother, the typical underpaid school teacher, supported the family. In the evening she would prepare tomorrow's lessons, reading student papers, always with Benito at the same table on the chair at her side, carefully scribbling in his notebook. He would proudly display the large printed letters of his efforts and she would lift her head and smile. The perfect son. His mother's boy. The child of the bourgeoisie.

Years later the fascist Mussolini would say with pride: "The fact that I was born among the common people put the trump cards into my hands." When in actuality the tyrant was born and raised in the petite bourgeoisie, the class he spent the greatest part of his life condemning.

✦✦✦

I never thought of history when I shot Mussolini. The moment wasn't my moment, but his. His last. I was merely performing a service, balancing the on-going equation of actions and reactions. His betrayal had to be punished.

✦✦✦

I believed in his bombastic socialism. On the surface he was what we all needed at the time. A man of actions, a clear speaker, an exciter of ideas and of crowds. At twenty he was the personification of the true socialist revolutionary youth: truly passionate, impatient and hungry, completely out of control with savage discontent. And of course, an insatiable appetite for self-dramatization.

In 1902 Mussolini left Gualtieri for Switzerland to work as a rural school teacher. He left behind a soldier's wife, a beautiful girl of nineteen. He had brutalized her. Frequently subjecting her to beatings and the uncontrollable savagery of his lust. He would brag how he could do what he liked with her, making love violently, and selfishly. On one occasion when she displayed a preference to spend the night with her husband, in a blind rage he drove a pen-knife deep into the flesh of her thigh. I believe that the real reason he left for Switzerland was fear of retaliation by her husband or the authorities.

He wandered as a penniless worker, pockets empty except for a nickel medallion of Karl Marx.

His own political concoction, an idiosyncratic anarchistic socialist. The perfect entertainer. At twenty he perfected his appearance: posed as the seasoned revolutionary physically consumed by an inner intellectual passion. Hair thinning. Shaving only occasionally. A pallor maintained throughout the summer. And of course, the mandatory dark shadows under the intense eyes. Fired by visions of violent social change, he wandered the streets of Lausanne arguing, quarreling, making inflammatory speeches.

Angelica Balabanoff, a Russian socialist afflicted with a slight hunchback. A lover of the young Mussolini whom I met later in Turin:

> His philosophical views were always the reflection of the book he had happened to read last. He tried to absorb the whole history of political philosophy within a few months. Picking up ideas, and misinterpreting them. He found the most inspiration not in Marx, whom he found difficult, but in Blanqui, the violent French revolutionary and in Prince Kropotkin, the Russian anarchist.
>
> Every day it was the same, we would engage in violent sex, and he would practise his public speaking

on me: 'When will the day of vengeance come? When will the people free themselves from tyranny and from religion, that immoral disease of the mind?'

I was supposed to welcome his rude embraces and listen. 'Who was Christ, but a small mean man who in two years converted a few villages and whose disciples were a dozen ignorant vagabonds, the scum of Palestine?'

A neurotic, excitable, self-pitying, excessively blasphemous, vindictively revengeful, aggressive, poorly dressed sponge who hated manual labour and considered himself an intellectual. Who constantly complaining of his health and boasted of his virility. A man who seldom washed.

✦✦✦

The stone wall at Mussolini's back, the stone coldness in his eyes. My truth is memory. I spend my time inventing my memories. The room is distant, the objects disappear on contact. If I cannot touch my physical present how can I ever expect to touch my past. And what is this past but a story retold. How Claretta could hardly stand, how Mussolini supported them both, one hand against the stone wall, in their last walk. Is it true that I fabricate what pleases me and call it remembrance? The truth is my telling; what I tell cannot be false. The absence of speech is the only possibility of falsehood. Silence is the great thief of reality. If I told you Mussolini broke down and wept, crumbled to the ground begging for mercy as I aimed the gun, it would be true. That he stuck out his chest and said aim for the heart would be the lie if it was not part of my telling. History is such that all which I relate is irrefutable truth.

Honesty of course is an entirely different matter. I don't know honesty. I don't think I've spent more than twenty minutes without contradicting myself. Mussolini never contradicted himself, he lied, told you one way and acted the opposite. Said what he did was for the people as he sent them to their unheroic deaths. Hypocrisy is detestable. All hypocrites should be made hunchbacked and wart-faced to reflect externally what is hidden away inside them.

Don't ever confuse contradiction with hypocrisy.

The boy is looking over the meat on my fork. He knows the correct answer is silence.

◆◆◆

It was raining. I didn't think they would let me off the boat. There were rules I did not understand. I was asked so many questions. There were so many pieces of paper to be filled out. I had status for the one term I had served in the Socialist government after the war. But I thought they would be angry — my shooting of the tyrant was in direct opposition to the wishes of the Allies. They wanted him alive, they wanted information, a trial for his crimes. But we all knew he was guilty. There was no need to waste any more time listening to his lies. What a great speech he could have made during the trial. And all those documents he valued so highly. Especially the briefcase of letters from Churchill. Just more diplomatic falsehood. Sure there were no death camps, but there were the political prisoners and the disappeared. There were many of us who died in open gun-battles with his troops. He betrayed us — not just us, his old comrades, but all of the Italian people. Sold us wars we could not win. There were some of us who never cheered him in the square. For us there was no question. He deserved death. I agree that the socialists should have exercised more of an armed struggle in the summer of 1920. First during the Milan and Turin strikes. But most in the autumn when the fascist squads began to carry out raids on behalf of the landowners. His attacks were ruthless, crushing our skulls with the butts of his rifles in an effort to end our socialist ideas. Aiming at our hearts with his midnight rifles to break our socialist spirit. For the murdered editors from *El Lavoratore* alone he deserved the death sentence. If only we could put on trial the industrialists who paid the fascists to destroy freedom. That would have been the trial worth the effort and expense. Not his.

The capitalist custom officials knew my identity. My visa for entry was still pending in the US, so without prior application I was attempting to enter Canada. Here in one of Churchill's colonies merely one more immigrant who professed not to speak English. One more dumb immigrating peasant, a displaced person, or DP as we were called on the streets of Toronto. Dumb prick. Stupid DP. One more cheap labourer to build a glorious new capitalist society after the war. A time of prosperity. Of victory. One more wop was coming to Toronto to excavate the subway, to build the new homes for the returning heroes. Why not let this factory worker and freedom fighter into the Dominion of Canada? There was no mention on the application, there was no appropriate space in which to declare that one had executed a tyrant. The lie of silence is more difficult to detect. I did not inform them that I had been elected to the Socialist Parliament after the war. Nor did I remind them of my numerous public addresses, where my political theories were tolerated while my prowess with a machine gun was cheered. Why complicate the issue? A man's past can disappear on the long trip across the ocean.

I told them my name was too hard to remember in English, so they let me in with a shorter new name.

My cousin Benito (a small irony, but one not worth remembering) was working on Toronto's first subway line. My job was easy. They gave me a pick and an area of rock and earth to strike. I would loosen a small area, rest while someone else shoveled the results of my effort into a wheelbarrow, and begin again. And on until the lunch whistle blew. For weeks. From six in the morning until four in the afternoon. I was no longer a young man. At first I slept on a cot in a room with three of Benito's whimpering, screaming, obnoxious children. Within a few months I had my own room. The blisters on my hands quickly became calloused and my strained muscles hardened. In the first six months I must have raised my pick six million times. I chopped and thought. And this is precisely the problem which occurred.

I had escaped my past by successfully entering a new country and identity. For a short period I was able to forget who I was and assume the identity of the peasant labourer, the contented alienated labourer, the exploited who derived his strength from his pay cheque.

But the mechanical work, instead of lulling my brain into an anaesthetized state of complete subjection, gave me time to think, to remember. It wasn't long until the work was torture. Not because of physical exertion but because of its inability to preoccupy my mind, to excorcize my memories. Each time I lifted the pick I was lifting my gun against Mussolini. This was not a new life but the reliving in an altered form of a struggle already ended. I grew more and more despondent. There was no choice. In the seventh month I quit. Retreated to this room. The money I had saved working was limited. The only choice was to dig into my reserves. No one would suspect now if I used it, some of the money I had earned during the final days of the war. There were still many questions about its disappearance so one couldn't be too careful. There were many Italian police officials still actively searching. I had to proceed with care in order to spend my share of the Dongo treasure.

✦✦✦

I am sitting at my table planning to write a letter. It has been all day. I sit here. First darkness. Light. All day. I don't move. Planning to write. Slowly less light. But what do I say to this man. And in my planning I hear at the door, I am sure it is the boy. Sitting outside the door. Waiting for me. But not today because I am occupied. Writing a letter to the pilot of the Enola Gay. And now it is darkness again as though it has always been darkness. So still. It is hours since I've even moved my hand. This stillness has become part of my industry, part of the writing of the letter, the planning. Obviously so much concentrated conservation of energy will force a sudden release — it is a physical inevitability. I want to write the letter. The darkness, the boy with his eyes on the door, the concentration of ears in the walls, all these will not distract me. Today I am a man of purpose. Soon I will find a piece of paper, and then a pen and the task will nearly be complete.

What does this man to whom I'm writing want to hear? Is it necessary that I consider his thoughts before I begin my own? He is probably lying in a small room. Alone with his moment in history, his one elevation. Now his life is a continuous stillness outside history. This is the fate of those who enter history without a true understanding of its difficult texture.

But history and I have been lovers. Almost understanding in the confusion of our affair; not understanding. History is not a monogamous lover, not constant. One may be led to expect another affectionate embrace and history will turn, suddenly turn into a rock with meaningless death resting at the first touch of its jagged surface. Or when one expects insurmountable resistance, stakes everything, covers oneself in heavy protections and thrusts head first at history: reaching the full momentum of your charge it will calmly change its grimace to a smile. Weighted you rush to its infinite bottom, the last great depth of absence. History can never be trusted to react predictably. Let this be recorded as the one fact of my understanding of this phantom lover, this two-tongued creature speaking softly of salvation while offering damnation. But even as I aimed my gun at Mussolini's chest, before I began to pull the trigger, a great roar was heard breaking through the enormous din of the moment. When I threw down the faulty gun, disappointment would have brought a lesser man to his knees. When my bullets finally tore against Mussolini's welcoming chest, history embraced me as the birth of its favourite child, the expected one. Silence became loud sustained applause.

◆◆◆

I wanted to know how he felt, what images pestered his days and nights — the man who pushed the button that released the one bomb on Hiroshima. My only image of this man is from a photograph taken just before take-off. His head protrudes above the body of the plane; he is smiling. If I can remember correctly, he is also waving, a friendly gesture to the photographer and the world. The name of the plane is printed in large letters below him on the side of the plane: Enola Gay. This name has become famous. I do not know this man's name but rather the name of his machine. They are in this instance both equal. It is not that the machine has been elevated to the status of a human but rather the man, by order of his government, been reduced to that of automaton. But later, after the event, it isn't the machine which slowly begins to lose its sanity, reflecting back on the grotesque destruction it has wrought, but the man.

I wanted to know if he understood any of the consequences of the event before he acted. I wanted to know if he considered himself an executioner, the fair hand of justice in punishment. I wrote him a letter.

> *Please forgive this intrusion by a stranger, but it isn't personal, I'm not so much interested in who you are as in what you did. You as an act of history, a decisive and destructive moment in history. The power which commanded you and your faithful response as a soldier I already understand. What I would like to penetrate is the man on the trigger — the person who actually administers death.*
>
> *You must not think this is merely a romantic indulgence.*
>
> *I presume you did not know the devastation you were unleashing. So in a sense you are innocent.*
>
> *Can you describe the feelings of guilt you possess as a result of Hiroshima?*
>
> *Did you understand the nature of the weapon?*

48

Do you feel it was necessary to drop this nuclear weapon on a populated area?

Do you believe it was a collective act of blood thirsty vengeance of the Allies?

Do you believe it was a racist action?

Are you proud to have participated in this particular moment in history?

You have no choice but to be remembered by this single event. If you could assist me with your response to the above inquires, it will be received with great gratitude.

Finally, when he did respond, he wrote:

I do not feel I was meant to take on all the guilt. I was merely acting as an instrument of my Country and God.

I was doing my duty.

In response to the question, which appears, if I understand you correctly, to ask if I feel any personal sense of responsibility for my actions.

I cannot answer your question directly: I am both unable and unwilling to do so.

I feel my best possible response is to forward to you a copy of an anonymous account sent to me from Japan two years after the war. One cannot help but read this account and feel a sense of grief.

Thank-you, for your consideration.

This was not a personal letter but rather a formal response with my name and address typed at the top. It is difficult to assess if this service was provided by Armstrong personally or by a military information service. The anonymous account read:

I was in the basement of the Fuel Hall searching through endless corridors of paper for a lost letter. I was on my hands and knees when I felt the tremor, or rather the quake of the ground. The light went out. I was struck on the head by either a piece of wood or a carton of papers. A stream of blood crossed one of my eyes. I awoke.

I had to get out.

I could see nothing.

Still on my hands and knees, crawling toward the stairs, I found they weren't there. Only rubble. Broken boards, plaster, fragments of tile. Trying to clear my way, something soft, wet, a body. I screamed. From above I was answered by other cries for help which quickly turned to tears. Trying to climb, again I was struck, this time by falling concrete. And then I heard it, the rushing water. The pipes had broken. I had to get out. I would either be buried in the rubble or drown in the rapidly rising water.

Dazed, bleeding, I climbed, crawled like a worm through the rubble. Clawing.

Until, without knowing it, I was standing on the first floor of the building. It was as dark as the basement. The whole area was covered in a thick black smoke.

The window and just outside the street, I jumped. Ran. Toward the Motoyasu Bridge. And as I started to cross it, saw a man with arms and legs pointing at the sky, naked, twitching convulsively. His armpit was burning. I retreated, ran down the stones to the river.

When looking back through the thick grey cloud, toward the Fuel Hall, I saw it suddenly burst into flames. The entire building instantly became a great fire. All the buildings were burning, the Promotion Hall, the Chamber of Commerce, the Post Office, had all ignited.

I sat on the stone steps beside the Motoyasu River bewildered, silent. My clothing in shreds. All my hair had been burnt away. My skin burned until large areas of flesh lay exposed. I was bleeding from the face and many other parts of my body.

Some of my fellow workers were also sitting by the river. All of us sat silent, staring blankly at the destruction.

The fires were beginning to spread. Trying to avoid the growing heat I moved closer to the water, but the water appeared to retreat at my approach. I moved closer.

The burning buildings sent out thick clouds of black smoke and shot great flames into the darkened sky. Scraps of red hot metal and burning wood rained down upon all those seated by the river. I could not look up, the smoke and heat were too painful to my already scorched eyes. Without warning the water at my feet began to swirl, a whirlpool, and then it shot upward forming a giant tower of water. I sat numb in terror. And then the water monster swam away.

Great drops of rain began to fall. It was no ordinary rain but dark and heavy and extremely cold. Wet, I became chilled. Shivering. I climbed the slippery stone steps and made my way to a burning building in order to warm myself.

Now dry, feeling somewhat better, I had to escape. I tried walking, but only with difficulty and pain. The smoke from the burning buildings was so dense I was guided more by instinct than sight.

I reached the next bridge, Aioi Bridge, but here the situation was no better. I had to escape the city.

Picking up a sheet of twisted tin I cooled it in the river and then held it over my head as a shield from the falling burning debris. I was walking toward Koi, at the far western edge of the city. My injuries made it impossible to proceed very quickly. And there were the constant detours to avoid the blazing buildings.

It was in hell that I walked. The entire city was one huge fire and I was inside the flames and black smoke. The dead, everywhere, lying as they had fallen. Shadows of naked bodies, bleeding and burnt, would cross my path. Our eyes could never meet. Driven, I pushed myself to continue.

By mid-afternoon, I had reached Koi. Trying to

explain the plight of my fellow workers sitting by the
Motoyasu Bridge to a medical soldier, I collapsed.

◆◆◆

This was nothing to me. A mere formality. Propaganda
with a humanistic perspective. What was I supposed to feel:
pity? Pity for the men suffering in the attack? Pity for the guilt
of the men who had perpetrated the attack? No. I felt only
propaganda, that I was the victim of the wrong answers to the
correct questions. Couldn't Armstrong answer for himself,
why did he have to continue to be a puppet for their wills?
Did he have nothing personal to contribute? But perhaps that
was precisely the explanation. I had put too much store in
Armstrong as the individual. He didn't push the button, release
the bomb, it was the machine: the name of the plane is better
known than the man who flew it. The plane and the men were
one, products of the great American assembly line. Parts of
another's will. Empty except as they responded in the proper
manner to the commands of their superiors. This was not a
man to whom I was writing; why then should I expect a
human, an individual response? A form letter was the proper
response. A humanistic account was the proper response.
Anything else would have been inappropriate. But still, I can't
help but see a person on the button.

The plane was a B-29, its wing span, its cruising altitude...
These men inside the Enola Gay were more important

than the machinery. Why did they allow themselves to be forgotten by history? It was not Truman who executed this mission but... no, possibly the response was correct. It wasn't men, but history which flew the plane and released the bomb. Possibly it wasn't men and women and children who died and suffered in the explosion, but history suddenly vaporized caught in the fireball; possibly it was history whose eyes melted as it watched the explosion.

HINCKLEY

On some days I stubbornly refuse to have any human contact. Adam knows I am inside. The boy hears the occasional sound as I strike a match, he smells the cigarette tobacco seeping under the closed door. Steadfastly I refuse my tray of food. I am not bored just sitting in the room alone. This is a day of absence. Tomorrow I will need company and the door may be opened.

◆◆◆

I think Hinckley is a bumbling idiot.

◆◆◆

My first meeting with Hinckley had been unexpected. One of those rare days when I could no longer tolerate the enclosure of the room, when all the points were closing in through an over-extended familiarity. When every detail of the room was competing for my attention.

I escaped to the park, to the enclosure of an open and unfamiliar territory. In the banality of standing in the centre of the park, at the water fountain, waiting my turn for a drink, a disembodied voice at the base of my neck. Flat damp words. A monologue from an invisible person.

◆◆◆

His eyes dull, no brightness; when looking at you, portraying not attentiveness, but absence. John's body might have been composed of putty; soft flesh and muscle hanging loosely on a slouching skeleton. All visible skin the colour of a larva, a specimen which shrivels on contact with sunlight.

When he began to speak, after my initial repulsion, I found myself leaning forward in an effort not to miss a word. I didn't attempt to perpetuate the façade of the illiterate immigrant unable to speak English, but rather I made an effort to respond to his tone of voice in a like manner. Here, obviously, for the first time in North America, was someone to whom I could relate. It was beyond me to understand why there was this affinity, what it was that attracted me. No reason I could discern. Why? I kept asking myself, why? Why

I, who had made such a significant contribution to history, should feel that in this insignificant boy there was any potential, any hope for our futures.

◆◆◆

Pretend

Pretend you are a virgin on fire
An outcast in the midst of madness
The scion of something unthinkable
Satan's long lost illegitimate son
A solitary weed among carnations
The last living shit on earth
Dracula on a crowded beach
A child without a home
The loser of a one man race
Rare meat thrown to a hungry lion
A faded flag on a windy day

Welcome to the truth
Welcome to reality
Welcome to my world

John Hinckley

+++

Sitting on a bench, one of the many forming a circle around the drinking fountain, John told me he was in Toronto to see his idol, John Lennon.

"Don't you think it's curious that both our first names are John?"

"Yes, I suppose so."

"Sometimes I think I am John Lennon. That if he hadn't been born first, I would be John Lennon and he would be Hinckley. Do you know what I mean? Our bodies would still be the same but the people inside would be switched."

He was staring at me, as close to an inquisitive gaze as he could construct on his soft face.

"Of course," I answered, appearing attentive. "Do you play the guitar and sing?"

"I try. Actually, I've only, so far, played for myself. In my room at home I've practised. My father told me once he heard me through the door and I was very good. It made me nervous to know they were listening. That's one of the reasons I've left home and gone on the road."

"Just to get away from home?"

"I also have a binder of songs that I've written. If I could only meet John Lennon and play them for him, there's no doubt, I'm sure he'd want to buy them. And he'd want me to play them with him. Sure."

He was drifting off. The conversation was deteriorating into what I later realized were his fantasy monologues. The critical element I ascertained about his character from this first meeting was that Hinckley wanted fame. He wanted to raise himself quickly from the gutter of life, from the pit of obscurity into the heights of stardom. He was dissatisfied with his life and wanted not just to succeed but to make a significant mark, to be catapulted to the top from below ground. Here was a perfect recipient of my awakening attention and my growing desire. Here finally was my instrument, if only I could hold and cultivate him.

Penetrating by slow jabs into the wall of his monologue, I was able, after considerable effort, to secure a response concerning a meeting with him the next day at the fountain. He agreed on condition he wasn't occupied with his friend Lennon. It was the best offer I could induce him to make.

♦ ♦ ♦

It took me very little time to calculate how to put Hinckley to use. As though I had been waiting these years for his arrival. Planning without understanding I had been planning.

My one action had been enough to make a scratch on history, but in only thirty years it was forgotten. Now I knew what had to be done with the money, the treasure that was my heritage. I could re-enter history by eliminating another tyrant. It was obvious to me that the President embodied the same potential for destruction as Mussolini. Both were perfect liars. Both could make the people stand up and cheer them in the public squares, while perpetuating covert actions of terror against those who might ideologically dare to disagree with their self-serving domestic and foreign policies.

Every day with my breakfast Adam brought a newspaper. In my room I judged them all, the ones my bullets hadn't reached.

◆◆◆

We were to meet in the park the next day. He was late; I began doubting whether he had the stability to remember an appointment, but an hour late was his standard deviation.

Sweat was emanating from every pore in my forehead. I was nervous, anticipating the complex path I had planned for this pathetic individual.

He looked completely dejected, as though everyone near to him in the world had suddenly deserted him.

"He wouldn't see me," he blurted out. "I waited. I waited in Lennon's hotel lobby before the concert. And when I finally saw him, I ran up. I was so excited to see...I could almost touch him. I reached out. One of his body-guards grabbed me by the collar. I waved the papers. But he just smiled. Saw me hanging and...I thought his...I wish I had a knife...I would have...it was horrible. I wanted to get to him. Hanging in the air. Horrible. He just let me fall. Papers everywhere...I was on my knees."

I consoled him as best I could. We sat on the bench, my arm around his whimpering shoulder. He kept repeating the story over and over again. With each repetition he became harder, the knife became longer and sharper, and his potential attack became more savage. I suspect he felt I was a surrogate father who could sympathize with his important problems.

So I explained I was Colonel Valerio the man who killed Mussolini.

"You...shot...Mussolini?"

"Yes." And I wasn't sure if he knew who Mussolini was, but that I had killed someone and was confiding in him was more than adequate.

Here was someone he could respect, who had done what he wanted to do today: kill the tyrant. And here was someone who was putting his trust in him, elevating him from a meaningless nonentity to the possessor of another's confidence, another's deepest secret.

So Hinckley was easily won. By the time he left Toronto later that week we had become partners in a conspiracy, we had formed a two man terrorist cell. Our one mission was to do justice. At this point I felt no necessity to reveal the final direction, the final action he was being conditioned to undertake. At this stage it was enough for us both that he was under my direct guidance.

When he left for California, for Hollywood, to try to sell his songs, we had made arrangements that he would phone me at least once a week from different phone booths, and charge the calls to his father's business account, where they would never be noticed, just one more in the numerous calls necessary to carry on a large-scale oil business. Letters were too dangerous — easily interceptable and evidence in a court of law — also, so difficult to write.

◆◆◆

The problem was how to develop Hinckley's potential. At the moment he was motivated by an undirected rage against anyone who stood in opposition to his latest impossible fantasies. Both the fantasy and the rage had to be directed to meet my needs. It was easy enough to make him want to strike out. On the telephone I once inadvertently told him a local music reviewer had written that John Lennon's latest album was terrible. He asked me if I would buy a small handgun and shoot the reviewer; he was too busy at the moment to fly to Toronto; an important deal was currently entering the critical stage of negotiation.

A plan was necessary which focused and extended the duration of his fantasy rage. I needed a tool by which to combine the fragmented nature of his temporary obsessions into a predictable pathological behaviour.

At first I thought it would be easy to direct his rage at a specific object. I would, during each phone conversation, articulate a list of negatives against the President. But it didn't fix in his memory. The next conversation was always the first he had heard.

Initially I presumed Hinckley was unable to concentrate;

he couldn't fix on one subject over an extended period of time. But each of our conversations contained a mention of John Lennon, demonstrating at least a singular ability to sustain one obsession.

✦✦✦

Troubling over this matter for a number of weeks, I finally realized his psyche contained an escape valve. All negative obsessions had a life span in Hinckley's memory of only a few hours. So much of his life was opposition, disappointment, failure, that it was impossible that he could simultaneously contain it all in his memory and hope to continue. Avoidance was fundamental to his survival.

✦✦✦

The only enduring obsessions he was capable of were positive fantasies. He was incapable of looking into the future unless there was a promise of reward. His plans never contained the contingency of negativity. Life was too negative for Hinckley to plan a future addition of negativity.

It was after this realization of the direction of Hinckley's need for positive fantasy directiveness that I invented *The National Front*.

I thought it would be impossible to train his mind to follow a socialistic analysis to political action, to revolution, to destruction of late capitalism. The effort and time to re-educate were impossible. Instead, I would have him love the man. Everything the President embodied John would want to embody.

He would never be able to kill the object of his hatred — he was far too weak. He was capable of killing only that which he loved.

This amorphous jelly wanted to become something important. Therefore, twisting the equation, I offered him the President.

Capitalism is the system of individual freedom. You can do anything to reach the top. The President has reached the top: he is success. If you want to succeed, to reach the top, kill the President. By killing him you become his fame. The two principal rewards of capitalism are money and fame. Once fame is achieved money easily follows.

It was necessary to program the soldier. I gave him a number of short, clearly written books advocating a capitalist fascist position. He enjoyed them. I gave him more.

We started a newsletter in which we were the only contributors and the only readers. Poetry and the short polemical article were his two favourite genres, but sometimes I would ask him to write a direct response to what I had just written and sometimes I would respond to his written piece. Since we saw each other so seldom the critiques had to be mailed. This was a necessary risk. *The National Front* was produced weekly, his indoctrination was swift; after a few months the training was complete.

He phoned me and said in an excited voice: "The President is a great American. The greatest of our entire history."

The next stage was to send him information about newsworthy assassins — an article about myself, a book on Oswald...

❖❖❖

I Read The News Today, Oh No!

*John Lennon is dead and people continue to laugh
and dream and live...
Oh, listen to the comedian tell his jokes...
The audience is laughing so he must be amusing,
but I'm not close to a smile. John Lennon is dead!*

*Seventy five thousand people with brains are
watching the all important football game...
Isn't it fun and exciting! No, no, no a thousand times.*

*For an entire week after the assassination
of John Lennon I cried like a sick baby...
What I cannot comprehend is the fact that
people are trying to carry on with life now.
What's the use?*

In America, heros are meant to be killed. Idols
are meant to be shot in the back. Guns are neat
little things, aren't they? They can kill
extraordinary people with very little effort.

John Lennon died a couple of weeks ago and I
did too. Bang, bang, you're all dead. The stupid
earth keeps revolving and the stupid people keep
the faith but they are actually walking corpses.
Everyone is dead.

John Hinckley

◆◆◆

He was shattered, devastated when Mark Chapman shot
Lennon outside the Dakota. His first love had been killed by
another.

In the middle of our phone conversation the news came on
his motel TV. The phone was left hanging in the air — I could
hear him yelling — No. No. No — over and over again while
he packed. In New York the same day standing outside the
Dakota, one of the throng in a silent vigil for themselves. At
the funeral he watched part of himself being lowered into the
past.

There were no phone calls or letters for three weeks, but
when he finally did call it was with more enthusiasm.
Lennon's death had left an angry gap demanding to be filled.

68

The President was waiting, ready made. How long could he remain in mourning, wallowing in the negativity of self-pity?

He wanted to know how to buy a gun.

"It is easy," I told him. "Stay out all night. Walk the streets of New York. Ask."

He said he had been out all night with some of the boys from the vigil.

"These are the wrong people. Find someone who knows the street and you will find your gun."

I thought it wouldn't be long now. I even started to feel quite proud of myself.

But what I hadn't anticipated was the development of Hinckley's other obsessions. Food. And then love.

◆◆◆

In our correspondence and phone communications there was no indication Hinckley was following any other channel for his destructive desire than the one I had carefully prepared for his consumption. The slight drifting of thought, the inappropriate silences were customary displays of his unbalanced character, not very strong indicators that I should be watching for a psychic competitor infringing on my scheme.

But the moment we met it was obvious. It had been only five weeks since our last rendezvous at the fountain; he had literally changed from a slightly flabby, stooped shouldered, pudgy-faced boy into a full-grown fat blob.

Hinckley had found food.

He had become obsessed with eating, trying to fill the emptiness which constituted his person with an easily consumable physical substance.

I tried not to look shocked but it was obvious.

"I've put on a little weight since the last time you saw me?"

At the current rate of expansion in one year he would be completely round.

"Yes, but, so quickly?"

"Is it that noticeable?"

He had to be placated, so I told him only his close friends would notice.

"Oh, there's not much to do when you're on the road. I try to get up before noon. The maids usually wake you anyway trying the door, wanting to clean your room. Then I wander over to the nearest McDonald's. When I take a hotel room the first thing I do is to scout the neighbourhood for the closest McDonald's."

"*The National Front* has just published a new issue."

"A double order of french fries, one quarter-pounder with cheese, a Big Mac and at least two milkshakes. Not much to do. Walk a bit. Play my guitar. For lunch usually at either another McDonald's or a Wendy's. Same as breakfast, maybe one less milkshake."

"I sent the President a copy of our newsletter. Do you think he acts like a fascist?"

"At seven or eight o'clock I find a self-service restaurant to have a few beers with supper. I like heaps of roast beef and mashed potatoes covered with gravy. A double apple pie and ice cream for dessert."

"Listen to me: there has to be more to life than food."

"I enjoy my late night visits to the all-night coffee and donut shops. I enjoy drinking coffee and eat donuts until three or four in the morning."

His patterns each day were basically the same — locales changed but not the frequency and the quantity of food.

His food obsession was a serious distraction. Something had to be done or all my previous efforts would be in vain.

◆◆◆

Hinckley has taken a room at the Carlton Inn at my expense. It is an expensive room with unlimited room service and a colour television equipped with home box office. When he phones he emits sounds of contentment.

Some days it's so absolutely slow, the brain, the eyes, nothing wants to open. These are the days I lie in bed, refuse to roll over, lie on my back and stare. A desire, a physical necessity to urinate suppressed — the extent of my involvement in life. The inevitable knocks at the door, unheard. I am not present today. No thoughts. Awake but not asleep. If biological tests were made, the rate of my breathing, my heart beat, would be shown on the verge of nonexistence. A physical presence, but a man absent.

When he phones at noon I am unable to negotiate the two feet to the telephone.

◆◆◆

It is an impossible necessity which demands each day something be accomplished. Days must also be passed in absence. These nonproductive passages of time are the touchstones from which the productive periods may be measured. Not the days of activity which are important but those of inactivity. One must practise boredom. It is not a state which comes naturally. Only with difficulty am I able to invoke its presence. How many times have I been engrossed in the demands of an activity and silently wished for the blanket of restful boredom?

◆◆◆

It can never be said that John ever ran completely on course; constant divergence was the essential construct of his personality. Phoning me at 4 a.m. this incoherent voice would stammer: "I'm in New York. Hungry. No sleep. No food two days. Money?" Or from Chicago: "Money? No room. Walking." With difficulty I would coordinate a location where he could receive a few hundred dollars. The banks are not cooperative in handing money to a fat madman who refuses to carry identification.

When I instructed him to go to the streets to find a gun, I hadn't meant him to live the life of the streets, to become one of the slime of the night, but obviously he had found a lifestyle which agreed with a dark cave in his personality. The creeps accepted without question this over-stuffed blob as one more charter member of their inferior fraternity and he reciprocated their degeneracy, an accepted peer.

There were never questions concerning what he did with the money, my interest was with the larger picture of the investment, not the specifics of any one allocation. Doubtless he squandered whatever I gave him on bodily indulgences, primarily food and expensive hotel rooms. No matter how little money he possessed, he insisted unequivocally on locating in an expensive hotel. It was either the streets, penniless, or the luxury of an expensive hotel room. Here he would import a large quantity of junk food, situate himself in front of the television and beside the telephone. During these periods of prosperity he would freely eat, watch television and make long-distance telephone calls — sometimes all three simultaneously. He had little concern for money. If it wasn't mine, it was his father's. If only he knew that I had half the Dongo treasure — the tyrant's booty to support my anti-tyrant operation.

"What are you eating?"

"I don't know, I think it's a Twinkie, but it's different, it's got more filling. I just had to call you. I saw the greatest movie."

"Where are you?"

"Washington. I waited outside the White House but I didn't see... I saw this movie — *Taxi Driver*. It's great. Travis is so real."

"What were you doing outside the White House?"

"It's okay. I was just watching. I wanted to see him. I didn't have any of the guns on..."

"Guns?!" He had advanced from planning to action. A major breakthrough.

"Yeah. I have two of them. I've been practising at a range. I'm getting better. But Travis. You should see him with those guns. They're on springs. And knives too."

The jelly had found a mould to fit. A hero had emerged. A positive image to emulate. This wasn't part of my plan but it didn't appear to be a hindrance.

Every time he phoned for the next month he described more of the movie, detail on detail — he had seen it at least fifteen times. He also explained how his target practice was improving — the instructor had actually commended him on his ability. Everything was looking hopeful until one of those late night phone calls:

"She won't see me. I left a poem."

"Where are you?"

"New Haven. I —" tears "— love her. Said she'd call the police."

Fallen in love.

Or rather fallen into unrequited, hopelessly impossible love. Not even romantic, but desperate masochistic romance.

The movie — he had it completely committed to memory. Knew every word of her dialogue, her screams, her tiniest gestures. Upon arrival in a hotel room his first duty was to unpack her publicity stills and carefully tape them on the walls. He loved Jodie Foster. The six pages dedicated to her in *People* magazine were her personal love letter to John.

She was not a prostitute, but yes, it was fun playing one in *Taxi Driver*.

The sweet young tart.

Jelly was developing shooting muscles sitting in front of the TV, a gun in each hand, shooting the screen: metal hitting metal.

Food was no longer as important. Travis was more concerned with tightening than with fattening his body. John had extreme difficulty with this aspect of the transformation: imitating the despair, the guns, the Knight Errant aspects was plastically simple compared to duplicating the episode in which Travis works strenuously on tightening every muscle in his body. Obviously this part of the film hadn't registered. It was only important to be quick on the draw, to be able to hit what he aimed at — he wasn't about to enter into hand to hand combat with the President. There was no need to practise running — no possibility of escape — and escape was antithetical to the plan. One must be caught and identified to be glorified.

Softness is a complete aesthetic system — those possessed by it refuse to abandon its embrace — it is the condition their bodies want and enjoy. They would no more part with their softness than give up living. Hardness is anathema to those who practise the vigours of softness. The avoidance of all bodily taxing situations is not easily accomplished. Diligent planning is necessary to avoid all physical exertion and uncomfortable extremes of temperature. Outdoor activity must be free of insects and possess only identifiable friendly wildlife. Physical challenge is unequivocally boring and especially unnecessary and therefore not natural to human life.

The jelly of John was in its proper place; he wouldn't have attempted to replace it for all other pleasures combined.

One of his love poems to Jodie dealt with his desire to protect her, to engulf her in the cushion of his softness.

His was the declared love of enclosure.

+++

Distraction, distraction. Why can't anything go according to my plan? He has stopped calling. No letters. Instead he is thinking of Jodie, writing her volumes of poems, letters, songs. Poor misdirected youth. Our newsletter has folded — *The National Front* has almost completely evaporated from his shallow memory. The tenuous fibres of this affection must somehow he kept alive and ready to be rekindled. It is only a matter of time before he becomes oversaturated with the love fantasy; he will need something, some hope to catch his fall. Three weeks since his last call.

This boy sitting across from me. Smiling. So normal. Bringing me his daily tray of food. So boring. No possibility that I could teach him to buy a gun, to shoot and love a president to death.

John has taken a small room not far from the Yale campus. Another student in his closet room hunched over a wooden desk. Instead of going to classes he studies her, following the object of his desire at a discreet distance.

✦✦✦

She wants so much to fit in, to be one of the normal students, not Jodie Foster superstar. No special status, just wants to go to school. And here is my delinquent jelly following her around. Her greatest fear come true — creeps outside every window.

Laughing with a couple of friends outside the lecture door and suddenly a chill runs through her body and the lips tighten — she felt eyes — a cold softness. Turning. Emptiness.

A body-guard would be too conspicuous. The studio would pay. Perhaps someone who looked more like a friend than a polyester jock. No. Only her imagination. No one is watching. Only the eyes of curious fellow students.

And Hinckley returns to his room to describe her infinite beauty in a song he will sing to her during their first date. Gathering his nerve and material to declare his love: he will phone her soon.

He sees nothing but the telephone. He sees only the telephone. There is no other object in the room. A direct link to his love object. Convincing himself that she waits at the other end for his call. How should he act?

"Hello, is this Jodie?"

"Yes."

Flabbergasted. He actually has her on the telephone. A

star. Talking to him.

"Jodie? Foster?"

"Yes. Who is this?"

"My name is John Hinckley, you don't know me, but..."

"Yes, I do!"

She knows who, me, my name.

"You're the one who has been writing those letters, those poems. I don't think it's fair. Why don't you leave me alone?"

"I thought we might meet, have..."

"Don't you understand? I don't know who you are. I don't want to know you. Please, please don't send me any more letters or phone me again. Good-bye."

She knows who I am, all he could think. The remainder of the conversation didn't register, not the intent or the specific requests. Sitting down at his student's desk to write her a letter. But instead, not even understanding why, he's on the telephone with me.

Finally.

I encourage him, try to build up his ego, tell him I just finished reading one of his poems, *Fascism 2*.

"It's excellent. I'm translating it into Italian. A paper in Rome wants to publish it."

"What...one of my poems?"

"With your permission, of course."

"Fascism? *Fascism 2*?"

Now there are only love poems; he has drifted so far away from my instruction.

"Do you need any money?"

One doesn't need money when one has love.

"No. I just called because... I just talked to... She wouldn't talk to me. But she knew my name."

"The President has announced his plan to put more missiles in Europe. He's such a great man. Don't you think so?"

"Yeah. But. I don't know if Jodie would like that. I wish I could talk to her."

✦✦✦

Slipping the letter under the door of her dormitory room, he walked quickly, not too conspicuously, down the corridor, around the corner and ran down the two flights of stairs.

The envelope addressed:

Jodie Foster, Superstar.

After hours of composition, the message scribbled, barely legible, filling one piece of writing paper:

Jodie Foster, love, just wait. I will rescue you very soon.
Please co-operate.
J.W.H.

It wasn't Jodie Foster he saw, was in love with, but the child prostitute, the character she played in *Taxi Driver*. He wanted to save her from the cage of corruption in which she was being held, and release her to the safety of his personal enclosure.

If only she would understand, she could live comfortably in his protection, they would be happy together, she could still do what she wanted but they would be together.

Leaving the letter he packed his bag and flew to New York. Two days later at 4:30 a.m. my phone rang. The voice incoherent. I couldn't understand a word.

"Call back in ten minutes. Get a hold of yourself."

The phone rang in five minutes.

"I'm better. It's just... I'm hungry. Haven't eaten today. And sleep. No room. Could you... I need to eat."

"Do you want me to send you some money?"

Everything was back in control.

"Can I come and visit?"

"Of course."

✦✦✦

John showed me his latest poem, it began:

The pain is sharper than a hypodermic penis.
Caught in a working meat-grinder.

It was signed: *Psychopathic Poet.*

Here was a sense of self-understanding which I hadn't expected.

✦✦✦

It was a till-death-do-us-part romance with Jodie.

✦✦✦

*Your hair is what attracts me, long and straight
and wavy in the right parts.*

*Your eyes are what attract me round and brown
and revealing the naked brow.*

*Your face is what attracts me sweet and cute
and capable of melting hearts.*

John

✦✦✦

Every day at noon we would meet by the fountain. It was obvious — there was no possible way to win him back — his love for Jodie was much more powerful than his love for the President. Whenever I mentioned our plan to shoot the President he would respond with enthusiasm about shooting

Jodie. Completely torn between two fantasies, combining elements of each until he had constructed a convoluted situation in which any action was impossible. He would shoot Jodie and then shoot himself. He would shoot the President and then Jodie and then himself. Too many directions. Frozen. Back and forth. Trying to find the best combination. Shoot himself and send Jodie the suicide letter. Shoot the President and then himself.

Until finally, after I had planted a small seed of an idea into the confusion of his thinking. He would shoot the President, dedicate the action to Jodie and so win her admiration and love.

The plan after this important decision was not difficult: we worked it out the same day. Tomorrow he would fly to Dallas and buy a gun. The following day to Los Angeles. Then take a bus cross country to Washington. There was less chance of being followed with this erratic itinerary of travel. No trail would be visible which led back to Toronto and my part in the conspiracy.

◆◆◆

Dallas was easy. He had some difficulty in answering why he wanted such a small gun, a .22, when the dealer had magnificent .38's, and larger, for not much more money.

He phoned from Hollywood.

"Phase one complete. I've purchased a ticket for

Washington. Phone on arrival."

And hung up abruptly. We were taking no unnecessary risks with our enterprise. I only found out later, in actuality John had purchased a bus ticket for New Haven that went by way of Washington. There was still the struggle between lovers, the unresolved question whether to consummate a union with the President or Jodie.

Four days and four nights in a Greyhound from Hollywood to Washington — from the home of the stars to where a star would be born, from the world of tinsel to the world of intrigue with hell between.

What firmness the jelly had developed became softer and softer with each bump and jar of the ride. Slowly, everything was becoming a blur. The landscape — there was no difference if he watched the asphalt or the distant horizon — was a homogeneous haze. Shadows were passed. Occasionally a grinning toothless face would emerge in the mist, hiss, coil its tongue and disappear. The sky would turn blood red, forcing him to close his eyes. In the blackness as the bus passed just outside so many nameless cities he could hear the sounds of battle, gun fire, explosions, see the fires, the burning cars and buildings, the sirens, the screams of pain, the cries for help. The bus rolled, bumped, swayed and his nausea grew. He began to spend as much time in the washroom as in his seat. Vomiting, diarrhea, sweat. The body trying to escape itself.

At every way station he planned to abandon the bus, but he was too lost, dispossessed of all drive and direction. It was always easier to return to his seat and suffer, to close his eyes and invoke sleep. He knew somewhere in the recesses of his psyche that he was on a holy mission, a pilgrimage and this suffering made his purpose that much more important, and there was an end, the suffering was finite, possible the next stop. Absent was any recollection of how long he had been on this bus, and of where and when he would be finally released.

He slumped in his seat, trying to hold the vomit inside his body between the bumps trying to write a poem. It was an ode to Jodie and the President. Finally they had become one. But after a few lines, long scratches across the page, the torment inside conquered this effort at mental stability and his vomit obliterated the text.

The motion disappeared. Another way station. He didn't have the strength to move, slouched, just another part of the seat. With his eyes closed it felt as though the bus was still moving. Just another food and toilet stop. They were all the same — identical furniture, faces, people, food. He felt it was a journey inside a circle, always the bus returned to the rest station from which it had departed.

A hand on his shoulder, shaking him. His eyes were open, frozen, fixed on the seat in front of him. Shaking him. A distant voice, very far away: "Washington. Washington, son. This is your stop. You asked me to tell you when we got to Washington."

Stumbling, crawling off the bus on his hands and knees. Like a snake slithering, twisting his body into a cab.

"The American Dream Hotel." He could barely speak.

"Never heard of it. Do you have an address?"

"It's... on..."

"Not in Washington. I know every hotel in DC and..."
"I mean...Park Central Hotel."
"Why didn't you say so in the first place?"

◆◆◆

Every day the same routine. Do you think it's easy? It takes discipline to set a course of action, or even to find yourself unexpectedly with a routine, and to continue it until boredom sets in and then still to continue. One of the most difficult of human activities is to sustain boredom, to endure its tortures and to preserve this situation. So each day that I perform my routine I do so by exercising my will. The continuity of my routine is not mechanistic in its repetition but passionate and wilful. I respect each moment for its purity, for what it is and not for what it isn't. With will against the resistance of boredom. Effort. Force.

I have no desire to change this table for any other table. I keep this table here with me. I expend more effort keeping it here than I would in its removal. Effort being an equation involving time and work. One act of removal does not equal years of its presence.

To be held within the confines of a very specific physical locale, to exercise the body only between four not very distant walls, this is the life of the room.

The decision of the room is a commitment. It is an old and venerable tradition. One which cannot be taken lightly.

♦♦♦

A block and a half from the White House in room 312 registered as Travis. The bus wouldn't stop; he collapses on the bed, closes his eyes and he is back on the bus. A shadow inside a shadow traveling through a shadow he falls into sleep. Tossing, turning — a difficult night.

Waking early. Wondering why he can't sleep. Turning on the TV. Cartoon outlines of figures chasing each other through outlines of landscapes, stupid actions accompanied by banal music. Talk shows. Only mildly interesting. Important stars talking with disinterested plastic male hosts. You wouldn't catch Jodie on any of those shows. Turns off the TV. Food. Walks across the street to McDonald's. One Egg McMuffin and a coffee. Times have changed; almost a Spartan breakfast.

Now the great decision has to be made, what to do. "What was it that, I ..." There were three alternatives. He felt terrible, even the Egg McMuffin was enough to make him run to the washroom. He could continue on to New Haven, shoot Jodie and himself and die in the headlines as a modern day Romeo and Juliet. John and Jodie.

He could go back to his room, put the gun to his temple, write a letter to Jodie explaining how it was entirely her fault, and shoot himself to die in obscurity as another statistic. He could shoot the President and become famous, known throughout the world, impress Jodie. But where was the President, how could he find him, get near enough? So difficult. Sitting for hours at McDonald's trying to decide what to do with his life. He could go back to the hotel and try to sleep. It would help to make him feel a little better. He decided in favour of attempting sleep — it was the option which promised the greatest likelihood of success.

In the hotel lobby, from a newspaper box he bought a *Washington Star*. Throwing it down with himself onto the bed, there on the page that fell open, a sign.

"This is it, this is for me."

The President's schedule for the day. Exactly where he would be and at precisely what time. There was no doubt. The decision had been made for him. He was now only the instrument. It was exactly noon. Another sign.

He had to cleanse his body for the ritual about to be performed. Standing in the shower, the cold water penetrating his body. No longer was he tired. His head was almost clear.

Nervous. Picking up the gun, his hand shaking so badly only with difficulty fitting the bullets into their chambers. Taking a Valium. One would not do. Three, or four. He had to be calm, he couldn't run. Never expected to be this nervous. Was he afraid of dying — would they kill him — they had killed Oswald, but that was a plot.

One more hour.

He still had to write the letter, the last letter, to Jodie:

Dear Jodie: There is a definite possibility that I will be killed in my attempt to get the President. It is for this very reason that I am writing you this letter now. As you will know by now, I love you very much. I feel very good about the fact that you at least know my name and how I feel about you.

Jodie, I would abandon this idea of getting the President in a second if I could only win your heart and live out the rest of my life with you whether it be in total obscurity or whatever. I will admit to you that the reason I am going ahead with this attempt now is because I just cannot wait any longer to impress you. I have to do something now to make you understand in no uncertain terms that I am doing all of this for your sake. By sacrificing my freedom and possibly my life, I hope to change your mind about me.

This letter is being written only an hour before I leave for the Hilton Hotel. Jodie, I am asking you, please look into your heart and at least give me the chance with this historical deed to gain your respect and love.

◆◆◆

Throwing the letter onto the desk — if he was successful the FBI would deliver it in person. Would be great to see her face, her reaction when she read the letter.

Everything moving so quickly. Placing the .22 in his pocket, and as he steps out the door placing in the other pocket of his coat a John Lennon button. Old dreams are never completely abandoned, merely placed in a hidden recess for safety, filed, on hold to be reactivated if the unlikely opportunity ever arises.

And there is the President waving at the crowd. The world racing. "He's looking right at me, this is the moment." But Hinckley is too slow, the events supersonic and the President disappears into the hotel.

Smiling, a plastic grin, innocent over-acted stupidity on his face, edging, twisting, sliding his way slowly into the press area.

"I'm so close. I don't believe it. Why doesn't someone stop me? Why isn't the Secret Service here? I was meant to. Travis never got this close."

It was a small well-behaved crowd and no one could be bothered with this foolish, overweight kid.

"I hope someone will stop me. It isn't fair. The President is a great man."

And suddenly he is coming out of the hotel.

"It's too quick. I'm not ready."

Taking the gun from his pocket as the President turns and waves at the crowd.

"They see the gun. People see the gun. Everyone is watching me. I can't do it. I have no choice. I have no choice. Forward to shoot..."

At the very last possible instant, the President almost safe inside his bulletproof limousine, Hinckley opens fire.

"It feels so good."

Six shots. All the practice paying off, the quick draws in front of the TV, the agonizing hours at the range until his trigger finger was sore. With each bullet a feeling of euphoria — the body returning to its natural state of jelly.

And they are on top of him. Arms, bodies covering him. They have the gun. Fists.

"And now they will kill me."

He's on the ground covered by secret service bodies.

"It's over. I've killed the President. We are both great men."

THE SHOT

What a minor scratch Hinckley was able to make on history. Bungler. The overweight moron left a trail leading straight back to me; he started telling them he was enchanted — that the evil sorcerer lived in Toronto.

I became totally crazed when I heard what he had done, or rather not succeeded in doing. Hinckley had failed. I had failed to kill the tyrant. Looking back, I now know something snapped. Even at the time I watched myself slide. I am in Como when we hear that Mussolini had been spotted on the run. An excitement.

"I saw you with him. The one who shot the President. Hinckley, he's the one I saw you with, in the park, you and him."

The boy had been following me around. I had taken him into my trust and he had betrayed me. The boy who entered my room daily had been a spy.

"On TV I saw him. I don't understand what you were doing with that man. He tried to kill the..."

How dare he question me. We had both lost all semblance of control. I reached out and slapped the boy across the face.

"Shut-up!" I screamed. You are in no position to question my authority.

I had drawn blood. He was silent.

"How dare you accuse me of betrayal. I've always fought against tyranny. It is you who are the traitor."

I had struck too hard. I had drawn blood. His cold eyes stunned, frozen. He wanted to elicit sympathy from me, his face going soft, his mouth slack. What compassion should I display for his betrayal? Too many of my friends died at the hands of his secret police, too many times we hid in fear from the madness of his vengeance. No, I have no compassion for his tyranny.

"I have been instructed by the Italian Communist Party." Taking my gun from the drawer beside my bed. He now knows I am a passionate anti-fascist. "Murderer. That's who you are. Blood. Blood. That's all you are." He backed up to the wall. He refused to plea. His eyes, his expression suddenly hardened. We were both resolute.

I aimed the gun at his chest. So many acts of treason would soon be accounted for. The gun jammed. I tried again: it went off: he fell forward: one bullet in his heart: he was dead.

If only he had not failed. If only the President had not escaped.

I closed the door. What had I done? Why did I repair my gun? It had become clear, the boy on the floor was too young, he was alone, too thin. A mistake. The correct end to betrayal, but the wrong body. The crime of curiosity did not match the severity of this punishment.

I checked his pulse, his breath on a mirror. A puddle of blood was forming on the hardwood floor.

It was noon. No one else would be home until 5:30. As long as no one heard or questioned the shot I would be safe. I could not reverse the bullet. Nothing to be done. No retraction was possible.

The phone rang. Impossible. No one.

"Hello?"

"Is this the residence of Walter Valerio?"

"Yes, but he isn't in at the moment, would you care to leave a message?"

"No."

Hung up without waiting for an answer. Only minutes before they would be at the door. Hinckley had talked. Someone heard the shot.

From the drawer beside my bed I removed an envelope containing a Canadian passport under a false name; $85,000 in Canadian and American currency.

I did not hesitate.

Locked the door. The body safely out of sight. Walked as quickly as possible to a busy street, to disappear into the crowd. A taxi. "The airport."

"Which terminal?"

"One."

I looked at the board. The next outgoing flight was in fifteen minutes to London. Too soon and the English customs officials are too snoopy. Lisbon in thirty. Perfect. Who would ever look for me in Portugal.

I never left the airport in Lisbon. I could feel them on my trail. The CIA or the FBI. Hinckley told them I was going to Lisbon. The boy wasn't dead; he overheard me talking to myself.

I took the first available flight to Faro in the Algarve; from Faro to a smaller town, Quarteira. Who would be looking for me so far south. Traveling light, just another tourist.

In Quarteira, nowhere, dressed in short pants and a beach shirt, this is where I've been for the last two years. No one followed.

I've abandoned the small room. I now live in a small apartment, two rooms, my own bathroom and a kitchenette. The living room is connected to the balcony by a wall composed of sliding glass doors. Here it is all air and light. The outdoors intrudes on the inside.

Since the balcony catches the morning sun, it is here that I sit and read the newspaper. The name Hinckley has not been mentioned in over a year. The case is closed; history has too many new incidents to bother recalling a failed attempt at assassination. The President persists.

My new world came fully furnished: a circular wooden dining table, brown, covered by four straw placemats and surrounded by four wooden chairs, brown and beige; a brown couch; a relatively square wooden coffee table, brown; two armchairs too poorly designed to hold a human body, brown; a wall unit with bookshelves and drawers surrounding the couch, brown and beige; a wooden cabinet, light brown;

linoleum floor tiles, light to dark brown; and smooth beige walls.

They have thoughtfully provided one piece of wall decoration — a painting of a horse. This painting never seems to escape my vision no matter where I sit in the room. For over a year I've planned to take it down, but it eludes me, consistently remaining in place. The horse is centrally painted, a view from the rear — the foreground therefore consists of its white tail in motion — the one active gesture in the entire canvas. The horse, rendered in tones of brown and beige, stands erect and square with his head cocked to the right, staring proudly into the painting's background at two small white horses who return his gaze. There are no anatomical clues, but I have grown to presume he is the male and the two smaller horses are his mares that he guards and after which he lusts. It is carefully framed in wood, gold and brown. It is not even an original painting but a photo reproduction of a mediocre work.

I am merely a tourist in this room, another one of the multitude who have come to this Portuguese beach town for the sun and food. If I removed the painting I would alter my status to resident. Each day here is my first and my last.

A tourist town is a perfect locale in which to hide. Here no one is taken seriously — their stay is of course only temporary and of no great importance. Although my daily activities have become almost regimented, meeting the same individuals at approximately the same time and location for months on end, no one has ever displayed the slightest sign of recognition. Each day I am a different tourist. It is quite inconceivable that anyone could have spent two years as a tourist in this one locale. No one has heard of my limited loci theory — the expansiveness of the finite area — which I find agreeable, providing me with a safe disappearance in presence. The perfection of my ideal, an almost invisible existence.

It became a habit to visit the beach every day.

◆◆◆

I don't mind seeing him, the boy's probing inquisitiveness might be the distraction needed. Hinckley phoned last night, three or four a.m., incoherently whimpering, complaining they were following him. My only advice, since he had absolutely no idea who they were, was to take a taxi to his hotel room and lock the door. My last instructions, phone me on his safe arrival at the room. The call hadn't come and its imminence had prevented my return to sleep. Today when the boy started cautiously asking his questions, I didn't complain. A willing historian.

"We had him on the run. The workers had taken Milan's suburbs, the Americans were advancing quickly and the Germans were in full retreat. By blocking the two main roads into Milan the partisans had effectively stopped the Republican troops from re-entering. The victory was ours. Mussolini had no choice but to run to Como.

"Is this when you stopped the truck?"

"Listen."

"I am just trying to tie it all together. Sometimes I don't know quite where you are...the connecting..."

"It's obvious. It's enough that it occurred linearly. All I can give you are parts. If you want a description of history — listen."

"But, just one thing. What about the Dongo Treasure?"

"We didn't call it that — the anti-communists labeled it the Dongo Treasure — it was Mussolini's hoard. He had saved it for his escape. It was obvious months before he was actually forced to run that all hope was lost. Tried to lie. But it was clear — one look at the man. Depressed. All his energy dissipated. A broken man. His stupid last self-deception — to make the final stand in the mountains, his famous last command:

"'I shall go to the mountains. Surely it's not possible that five hundred men cannot be found who will follow me.'

"Not a chance. No one wanted to make a desperate symbolic stand dying for his lies in defeat. No last stance. But he did go to the mountains. Our sources told us Mussolini was en route to Como, on the road from Milan — in a small convoy of three trucks and two cars.

"Twenty kilometres from Como we spotted a convoy. We were dug in watching the road, three of us, expecting our contact. We had to decide quickly whether to attempt an attack against so many, when one of the trucks suddenly pulled over to the side of the road. The driver waved on the other trucks when they slowed to inquire if assistance was needed. The driver said something to satisfy their curiosity.

Mussolini never noticed the absence of one of his trucks until Como: too late.

"We quickly worked our way behind them. They were bent under the hood working on the truck's engine — they barely had time to see our faces when we opened fire.

"There was nothing wrong with the truck — these two fascists were merely pretending to fix the engine — giving themselves time until the others were safely out of sight — they hadn't expected partisans to discover them so quickly. Thieves stealing from thieves stealing from a thief — what honour is there among thieves except to steal? Mussolini's treasure was now ours."

"The Dongo Treasure."

"I have no precise catalogue of what the truck contained. There were hundreds of documents, bags filling more than half the truck, and goldbars, paintings, small sculpture and a box containing foreign currency. We decided to divide the treasure two ways — between ourselves and the Communist Party. The CINA could have the documents (most at least), the objects of art, all the gold bars (less three) and we would take the currency.

"Since my most recent job had been as an accountant, it fell to me to count and divide the money: 2,675 pounds; 2,150 sovereigns; 149,000 American dollars; 278,000 Swiss francs; 18,000,000 French francs. We each received one third. The gold bars we each buried separately — mine, hopefully, is still there."

"The documents, what were they?"

"So-called proofs of his innocence. He believed they

would help his defence in a post war trial. So-called proofs of what the Social Republic had done to save Northern Italy from the German desire for blood and slaves. Sure, I read some which showed his arguments, his disagreements with the Germans, but who was their partner, who sold our country to their caprice? There were documents he thought would appeal particularly to the American capitalists, how he had fought Communism. We had never wanted war — Mussolini betrayed the socialist movement when he turned his back, when his Revolution found bayonets and forgot bread. We were the first to fight Mussolini, when he was only a thug for the industrialists, and we were the last when he was a thief on the run.

"Documents — there were the two large brief cases I found with him at the end. More half-truths. Letters from Churchill, Umberto, Hitler and the trial at Verona. What did they prove? Nothing. That the tyrant could have been a worse tyrant. Nowhere was there innocence. Only the minor suggestion of a man who had become bored with blood, who wanted peace after the battle had been lost. I'm sure the documents his secretary threw into Lake Gouda from the launch on the eve of Mussolini's flight from Milan would have shown more of his blood-letting side.

"Documents. There is always one to prove your point.

"History shouldn't be written from its residue, censored, sorted, scientifically approached — there can be no science of real history. "

◆◆◆

It's not bad being bourgeois; after all the years of living in the darkness of one room to come outside, to live outdoors.

A fairly rich diet — not something you would want every moment of every day, but an occasional treat, alright.

◆◆◆

Heads, why do they have to be so persistent? Headaches. Waking with the dull throb. The least sunshine — a hammer. Why can't heads be as inconspicuous as toes — cut their nails and avoid protruding objects and there will be no disturbance. And the fog — when you think this thin film covers all possibility of clarity. So unpredictable, completely unreliable — one day ease of invention, and the very next, recall is torture. One drink too many the night before and the next morning a disaster of disturbing sounds.

I'll never figure it out: why do I have to try to figure it out? If it was up to me, I wouldn't bother. Obviously there's no answer. So just by beginning, failure is implicit. But if it's only a critique, not an answer, at least here, there is some logic to continue.

Colateral cooperation.

But what is the system from which I launch the critique, if it is not something it necessarily must be another thing, thought. And constantly taking all the moments, adding, history, trying to understand, fitting it together — the fragments, as much information as possible. Asking, trying to understand.

I would be just as content to leave it alone, but it won't leave me alone.

I lie down at the beach: I am in many ways content. This is supposed to be a socialist country. Here at the seaside resort it is very comfortable. Not luxury in the sense of opulence: accommodation is reasonable, food is fresh fish and vegetables, inexpensive. I have seen no signs of oppression or violence. Your typical tourist economy, merchants and purchasers, service industry and the served. Is the Portuguese family which runs the supermarket exploiting or is it being exploited?

Why do I bother to go on. Rambling. Impossible. If the boy wants one more answer today. The boy is dead. Some days I have such difficulty with time. Just lying here on my blanket in the protection of the parasol. Everything here is so absolutely slow; I think that is just the point — I ramble. The sun slows everything down, including the connectives.

The beach is a very scenic locale; everyday there are new people to entertain my vision. For 100 escudos the tanned, barefoot concierge gives me a canvas covering stretched between two wooden poles embedded in the sand — this is my shade. The canvas and my blanket constitute my outdoor apartment: a very airy room. Just the opposite sort of accommodation to which Ezra Pound was subjected. I am situated about fifty metres to one side of a large blue ball — about ten metres in diameter — balanced on a blue pole, supported by a netting of rope — labeled NIVEA Solar. I apply their cream to my body daily, their strongest formula, #7, ultraprotteccao.

It is my well-considered opinion that the sun is not my friend but a deadly adversary. I respect his strength. I wear a hat and sunglasses constantly. The one time I neglected to wear sunglasses his attack burst a blood vessel in my right eye, turning most of the eye's white area deep red — it didn't hurt but it was large and frightening looking. Passing from my indoor to my outdoor apartment, from here to the water and back are the only times I expose myself unclothed to direct sun rays. After two years on the beach I still have a slight pallor.

A Portuguese woman and her three small children have moved in on my right side. She is very loud, continually commanding the children who run back and forth to the water carrying shovels and pails of sand and water — practising I presume to be landscape gardeners or bricklayers. Their portable radio has been hung from their canvas roof and fixed on full volume tuned to no particular station.

In front of me are two sets of couples. One is young, mid twenties, German, lying on their towels directly in the sun. They hardly ever speak and are constantly applying Nivea lotion, with all their energy devoted to tanning. By three in the afternoon their bodies are obviously red. The other couple to the left are elderly, British, carefully hidden in the shade of their canvas covering. They talk politely, eat fresh fruit and have moderate tans. This is the beginning of their third sensible week on the beach.

Tomorrow the bodies will change — I will undoubtedly be here but they will be somewhere else and others very similar and completely different will have replaced them for my visual amusement.

A political, historical understanding is so difficult to achieve.

In the last few months I have limited myself to one ice cream cone a day.

◆◆◆

Sand and grease and salt. Some days I can't stand this foolish tourist town. Sand. I can't get rid of it. I think my body has begun to grow sand — it sprouts from every pore.

And grease. My sunglasses are foggy. A mist of grease over my sight.

And salt. I must be developing a thyroid condition. Every breath is saturated with salt.

And the sun.

There are days I just draw the drapes and return to bed with the lights out. And still I can feel it, sand in the bed, somewhere in the sheets.

◆◆◆

The last German betrayal.

Mussolini should have been more forceful in Milan when the Germans insisted on providing him with an escort of SS soldiers commanded by a Lieutenant Birzer. He was going to the mountains for Fascism's last battle and the Germans had already spiritually surrendered Italy to the Allies.

Waiting in the mountains for Pavolini to arrive with two thousand Blackshirts from all over Lombardy and from as far away as Turin and Alessandria. Raining. Holed up in Grandola at the Miravalle Hotel with a few ministers, Claretta and her brother, and his German escort who were guarding him as one would a prisoner. Waiting for Pavolini, sorting his documents — carefully marking those which dealt with the negotiations between the Ministry of Foreign Affairs and the Swiss Government concerning safe passage for his Government officials and their families. If the last stand failed, Switzerland was within an hour's drive.

Pavolini finally arriving in the rain in an armoured car from Como. The water dripping down a white face.

"Your Excellency. The Blackshirts in Como have signed a surrender with the partisans. I was only able to bring a few men."

Mussolini anxious: "How many?"

Embarrassed, he couldn't bring himself to answer.

"How many? Tell me."

"Twelve."

What a wet and miserable afternoon. It was the end. No one remained. The German jailer, Lieutenant Birzer, arranged that the defeated tyrant and his few remaining followers join a German convoy, of about forty trucks commanded by a Lieutenant Fallmeyer, retreating north along the lakeside road toward Innsbruck.

Pavolini in the armoured car:

"I'll shoot my way through any road blocks, the partisans won't stop us."

Mussolini driving his Alfa-Romeo, completely despondent, mechanically allowing himself to be led. After a few kilometres pulling over to the side of the road and entering the armoured car with Pavolini. Dragging two leather bags of documents with him.

Less than ten kilometres north of Menaggio the convey halts — an enormous tree trunk and boulders block the road. Shots. Two machine guns hidden in the mountains are firing on the armoured car. Pavolini returns their fire. A partisan is killed. And a white flag is frantically waved from behind the tree trunk. Three partisans approach the convoy.

And here again, Mussolini, you were a fool to trust yourself to the Germans.

Details. Why do I bother to give you so many details? Who cares to remember the names, the specifics of these events? It is nothing more than my conservatism being manifested.

"No. History without names and details is nothing but a fiction."

"History is always a fiction."

"But with the addition of these small details it appears truer."

"And therefore is a greater lie, for every name mentioned ten have been arbitrarily omitted. It is a random selection. Without the presence of this rabble there would be no history, no events and yet in my telling I exclude them, forget their presence except as background — to include each of them individually would be to clog the telling in infinite detail. Randomly I select details."

"There is no other choice."

"Possibly, but it isn't less unfair."

"Rather an excuse to be able to continue, which is fair enough."

"And that is all you ever want from me... to continue the telling at all costs... the story, true or false as long as I continue in the telling, fascinating you with an exciting narrative. But not all of it is interesting and what we deem not worthy of relating we exclude from telling and so soon forget."

"Of course."

"If one was to relate all of history as it occurred the telling would take as long as the events and all future life would be occupied with the living of a story told in the present."

"And so there would be no story, only the tangle of history rather than its excitement."

"And so always the lie in the name of expediency and clarity."

"Clarity."

"Why do I bother with this attempt at relating this false history? What good can it do you?"

"What harm?"

"To believe lies must be harmful."

"But to be completely ignorant, to have only silence, no history, no memory, isn't that much worse than an honest attempt. Your intention is not to lie..."

"It is an intricate part of all telling, but at least I lived the events I'm trying to relate — the distortions are part of my memory and my ability to render the experience in words."

"But were you with the partisans who stopped the convoy?"

"No, I had been ordered to Milan by the Committee of National Liberation and the Volunteer Freedom Corps to participate in a strategy meeting on the new terms of the armistice."

"It's obvious then why you're having difficulty relating this part of his capture."

"But it's important, it portrays how up to the very end Mussolini, despite his protests to the contrary, trusted the Germans and how they, up to the very end, were merely using him."

"Your story has only hinted at this condition, possibly..."

"The partisans told the German officers that to save unnecessary bloodshed they would allow their soldiers through the road block, but their orders were that no Italian Fascists could pass. Fallmeyer could easily have shot his way through, there were only a half-dozen partisans, but not putting much value on Italian Fascist life he negotiated.

"Free passage for the German trucks was traded for the Italians.

"A feeble attempt at hiding Mussolini was made. He was to put on a German soldier's overcoat and helmet and hide in one of the trucks. The final catch in the betrayal, unknown to the Fascists, the Germans and the partisans had arranged for a final search of the trucks at Dongo.

"Pavolini tried to put up a fight but was soon wounded and captured.

"Mussolini's capture was pathetic. A half hour after the inspection of the truck began in Dongo, a German soldier was found who appeared to be either drunk or asleep, squatting beside two barrels of gasoline, wearing large dark glasses — a machine-gun between his knees. The soldier at the rear of the truck was removed stumbling, and the Germans were allowed to drive on in search of safety.

"Mussolini was taken to the Mayor's office. Throwing the helmet and the German overcoat to the floor, declaring with disgust: "'I never want to see a German uniform again.' Cynically: 'That's my fate, from dust to power and from power back to dust.'"

"Walter!"

♦♦♦

I don't always understand, he rambles — right in the middle of a conversation about politics there will be this story about Mussolini. Some parts I've heard five times before, especially where he shoots, the gun jams — that really bothered him. And then, I'll be sitting there watching him eat, it's become a custom, and he'll flash on a new part — and usually it's worth all the waiting. And once he starts, its a nursing process — coax him on with nods, smiles, "oh yea," and some questions. I have to be careful with the questions. Best if it's a monologue — he just talks, remembers, hardly noticing I'm there. But sometimes he'll just go dead. Not a word. Then, I've got nothing to lose — might as well try a question. Its a test of his mood. If it's bad, that's it — "out" — I can hear him scream — "leave me alone," something derogatory — "idiot," or whatever. I've learned not to bother trying to stay, and not to say anything — just leave. Never mind the tray — he'll find it later and leave it outside the door.

◆◆◆

Yesterday. He hadn't said a word in ten minutes. So I asked him: "It was just something I was thinking. Do you mind if I ask?"

No answer.

"It's just — do you think everyone betrays someone sometime in their life?"

In the middle of a mouth full of food he stopped chewing, as though I had pushed a button. Spitting his food onto the plate.

"I've never betrayed anyone in my entire life. How dare..."

"I wasn't talking about you...it..."

"You have some nerve coming in here and acting the grand inquisitor with me."

Lost. One of those days. Wrong suggestion, wrong question. As I stood up — why not — a little mischief. "But what about Mussolini's money. Wasn't it suppose to go to the Communist Party, you..."

I was out the door and down the hall. He was standing at the door screaming: "Insolent."

111

◆◆◆

I wanted to talk with him today, at least listen, but nothing. No answer at the door. My knocks answered by silence. Calling his name — no response.

Leaving the tray by the door I retreated out of sight around the corner and sat on the stairs. Half an hour and still the door remained locked. As silently as possible, slowly I crept down the hall to the door. Listening. Trying to control my breathing. My ear against the wood. Nothing. Bending, trying to peer through the key hole. Darkness. And with my eye in the key hole — suddenly a hand fell on my shoulder. I would have shot straight up in the air if the weight of the hand hadn't held me in place. I think I emitted a muffled scream — the sound an animal makes when hit by a car — dead before the cry has left its mouth.

On the wrong side of the door. I was dead. Caught. But he just sort of pushed me to one side, unlocked the door and went in.

"Aren't you going to bring my lunch?"

I picked myself and the tray off the floor, hesitated slightly, not sure whether to run or enter.

"Come on boy, I'm hungry."

He was toying with my fear; he knew I feared him. Placing the tray on the table, I turned to leave.

"Sit."

I sat.

"What's wrong. No questions. Someone cut off your tongue?"

And he did laugh. My only question, and there was no way I was going to ask: where have you been? I couldn't take the chance. I just sat there in silence, wondering.

"I was in Milan when word came that Mussolini had been captured."

Why? What happened? Why was he out?

"At first, during the night, the Committee of National Liberation, decided to give me — Colonel Valerio as I was known to the partisans — the mission of bringing Mussolini back to Milan. But later, when there were only a few of us left at the meeting, we decided how to bring him back — a minor addition of a detail — dead. Palmiro Togliatti as head of the Communist Party and as Vice-Premier of Italy had ordered that Mussolini and all his Ministers were to be shot as soon as captured and identified. We didn't bother informing the non-Communist members of the Committee of our 'detail' as they felt bound by a term of the armistice that Mussolini should be handed over to the Allies. Did anyone believe we were going to give him to the Allies — he was our tyrant, our traitor and he deserved to die by our hands alone. Everyone suspected that our plans were a summary execution so there was great activity, a contest to find him first. Two American expeditions had failed. We tried a smoke screen, sending the Allied Headquarters at Siena a telegram informing them that we couldn't hand him over as he had been tried by Popular Tribunal and executed in the same place where fifteen patriots had been shot by the Fascists. I don't think they believed us. But they were kind enough to provide a pass which allowed me to circulate freely with my armed escort. I suspect they wanted to follow me to Mussolini.

"So armed with the Allied pass and another pass from the Volunteer Freedom Corps, a truck of twelve partisans, Aldo Lampredi and I in a small car in the lead left Milan. It was seven in the morning.

"An hour later we were in Como. I was excited. He was close — one could almost smell him. Running with Aldo up the steps of the Prefecture the first person I met was that coward Bertinelli — the new Prefect — puffed up with the authority of his new petty position. Demanding to see my papers — not satisfied with the one from the Volunteers, unimpressed until I stuffed the Allied pass under his nose. He betrayed the petty jealousies of a bourgeois spirit. I told him my orders were to take Mussolini and the other captured Fascists to Milan, but he wanted the credit of their capture for the local partisans of Como. Fools. Wasting time. I took out my gun and waved it violently in the air, forcing the cowards out of the room while I phoned Milan.

"Finally, after Bertinelli had been instructed by the Milan Committee to cooperate, we reached a compromise. They would hand over the Fascists if I signed a receipt for them and allowed two representatives from the Como Committee to accompany me. Afraid of losing their Fascist prizes. I had no patience for their petty desires for fame.

"Totally ridiculous when those two agents, two Italian intelligence officers, hired lackeys for the Americans, tried to follow me. Thought they could just attach themselves to the line of cars. I was furious. Tired of all these delays. When they pulled over for gas I waved my machine-gun and disarmed them — I was tempted to open fire — if they were American and not Italian I probably would have. What right did they have to try and follow me to Mussolini?

"Those stupid country fools, opening fire on my car as I drove into Dongo. Totally on edge. Thinking I had come to liberate their prisoners. Sure, but not to liberate them the way they thought. While they were still firing I jumped from my car and shouted that I was sent by General Command, waving my arms above my head.

"'Who's in command here? Take me to him at once.'

"Their arrogance was insufferable. Left me standing in the middle of the square for a half hour. And then that snot-nosed kid telling me the partisan commander was in the Town Hall. 'If the colonel cared to come up he would be received.'

"It took all my restraint not to slap his face with the butt of my machine-gun.

"'I gave an order. I intend it to be carried out.'

"Their commander, Count Bellini. A count, what were these fools doing, trying to re-establish a feudal system. We had won not lost the war against Fascism. He was determined to protect the Fascists. I presented him with a written order from the Milan Committee that I was to bring Mussolini to Milan, but he was cold, distant, refusing to comply.

"Exasperated I shouted: 'I have come to shoot Mussolini and the gerarchi.'

"And the only response he could provide to this honest expression was: 'Most irregular.' Like some petty British country gentry. 'Only this morning I made arrangements with the National Liberation Committee in Como to transport all the Fascists, including Mussolini, there.'

"'Your orders have been changed. Simple. Now where is Mussolini?'

"'Shooting them in Dongo? No. I'm the local partisan commander and I don't think I will allow it.'

"Finally, thinking he had found an excuse to delay me, he informed me that some of the Fascist prisoners were at Germasino, if I would wait here, he proposed to leave and get them. Anything to get rid of this fool. Only the Count and his two top assistants knew where Mussolini was hidden and he thought with his departure there was no hope I would discover their locale.

"He was wrong. Moretti and Canali, his two aides, were fervent Communists, in fact Moretti and I had fought the Fascists together. Within ten minutes of the Count's departure Lampredi, Moretti, Canali and myself were in a car heading out of Dongo."

◆◆◆

One of the strangest days was when he had the phone installed. The Bell man came to the door, a telephone under his arm, tools on a belt, saying he was here to install the telephone. But we already had one, there must be some mistake. No mistake, he had the proper address. And the name, it was Walter. I showed him up to the door and knocked. He was obviously waiting, the door opened instantaneously. The Bell man went in and the door was quickly closed.

A great mystery to all of us. What he wanted with a phone. Never in all the time I can remember had there been a visitor, only one or two letters — always official looking, from banks or something.

But despite our confusion, it was done within the hour. When I brought the lunch tray the phone was there, black, sitting on a small table beside his bed. I would have asked, but I saw he saw me looking and there in his eyes was the anger, that end-of-conversation disapproval, so I merely set the tray down and sat down.

He ate his food in silence and then I was instructed to leave.

It was late at night — early in the morning — the first day it rang. I'm not sure, but I think I heard a ring. I was sleeping — it could have been a dream — the thought had occupied my thinking all day, why not also my night. In the morning I resolved to stay up that night, a vigil, and listen — the mystery was becoming my central focus. Everything I didn't understand about Walter was now centred on his black telephone.

It was useless. I fell asleep on the stairs and my father had to wake me.

I tried the next night from my own room, sitting on the floor beside the bed, the door open, listening. I fell asleep and my father had to wake me — wondering, I presume, if I was ill, falling suddenly asleep everywhere but comfortably in bed.

◆◆◆

The phone rang. I'm sure of it. I'm not asleep. It's not that late. It couldn't be part of my sleep. If only someone would phone him before dark.

◆◆◆

Why was he in the park today sitting on the bench by the fountain talking to that creepy man?

I had to follow him. His door opened; I heard him lock it, he never did this if he was just going to the washroom. Didn't know I was in my room listening or didn't care. It isn't far to the park and when I saw him walking in that direction, especially turn left at the corner, it was easy. They greeted each other, almost, I'm not sure, as though they knew each other. It wasn't like the talks between us, they both talked, in fact, the other — who was he? — did most of the talking.

I wanted to get closer to hear what they said. Only one row of benches — just the fountain in front. Nothing to hide me. Too dangerous. All I could do was hide behind a tree. Lying on the ground facing them — nothing out of the ordinary — just someone relaxing by a tree. I could walk by them — just accidently be in the park getting a drink from the fountain. No. He knew me — I was supposed to be in school. Then he'd know I was spying and it would all be over.

They must have been there for over an hour. The ground was damp in the shade and I started to sneeze. Hiding behind the tree sneezing. When I finally stopped and was only sniffling, looking out, creeping a look — he was gone — they were both gone.

I ran. Not in sight. Which way? Must have gone home. I burst through the front door, heading for the stairs — heard his door close.

◆◆◆

I promised myself not to sleep all night. Couldn't use a radio or TV to keep me awake. Played solitaire, different games over and over again. Actually played out twice. And I did make it through the night, but there was no phone call. Nothing. What a waste. And I spent the day in bed sleeping — I think — I'm not sure — he went out again. Why couldn't I be waiting for that not the phone — never get it right.

Bursting. The curiosity about to explode inside me. I had to know — to find out. Had to. All I thought about. Couldn't do any homework. Hardly went to school.

◆◆◆

There was something — when he went out — those nights

the phone didn't ring. But when did the phone ring? And when I finally did hear it ring — three times — I could hear it before he picked it up. So what. I heard it, but who phoned? Who was he talking to — I had forgotten the real question trying to find out if anyone phoned — but of course they would — why else would he have a phone. He had to be talking to someone. If only it wasn't his own line — could have been easy just to pick up another phone in the house.

I tried the library under wire tapping but there weren't any books.

✦✦✦

When I brought his food — how could I ever control myself? How did I stop myself from asking? The man, the park, the phone. It was all too much for me. What was he doing? Would have given a year's allowance just for part of the answer.

Maybe if I didn't ask he'd tell me — just like with Mussolini. Time, but I had none, I wanted to know now, I had to.

✦✦✦

The knock at the door, lightly, somewhat frightened.

"Come in."

Nothing out of the usual, I was sitting at the table, calmly waiting. He set down the tray and sat down.

After a short silence, I started to talk about Mussolini.

"We found him at a farm house, one of our own, De Marias'. I'd used it once myself to hide out. An irony that they were hiding the Fascist here. I threw open the door to his bedroom, there he was, the tyrant standing, facing me. I didn't want to kill him here — this was the home of friends.

"'I have come to rescue you,' I said. 'Hurry.'

"All Mussolini could say, an ugly sarcastic grin on his face — he knew. 'Really. How kind of you.'

"'Are you armed?'

"'No.'

"And still lying in bed, her face to the wall, trying to hide like a child by closing her eyes was his mistress Claretta. It would have been so easy to have just lowered my machine-gun, but no, not here.

"'You too, get up. Hurry.' And she got up, shuffling slowly across the room to a pile of clothing, rummaging — I thought she was looking for a gun — I waved my gun and screamed: 'What are you looking for?'

"'My sweater.'

"Vain bourgeois fool to the very end. 'Hurry up. You don't need a sweater.'

"She picked up a handbag instead, and then another bag. Mussolini put on the grey jacket of his Militia uniform — a man who wanted to meet death properly uniformed — false pride to the last. Mussolini asked me for news about some of the others, but I was in no mood for his petty inquiries. 'We're looking after them.' He could only sigh as I forced him forward with the butt of my gun. 'Quickly.' Claretta grabs her coats, two, three, her wealth in furs. She can hardly walk in those outlandish high heels. Streaks of mascara. Eyes red.

"All of us in a row down the stairs, out of the house, down a steep lane to the car. Claretta holding Mussolini's arm tightly, for life, unable to walk, but he could barely support himself, using the wall as a crutch. Neither of them marching quickly to their death.

"I open the car door and push them into the backseat.

"'Get going, Geminazzo.'

"Moretti jumps onto the running board, Canali sits on the mud flap as we drive up the road to the Villa Belmonte.

"'Stop at the gates.'"

He just sits there. Quietly, listening, taking in every possible detail. There is something in the boy's face which I don't trust. I know he wants to ask me something, his expression is an open book.

"'Moretti get those people inside.'

"Mussolini and Claretta back up against the wall, stone at their backs.

"'In the name of the Communist Party I have been ordered to carry out the sentence of death against you for acts of treason and murder against the Italian people and the Italian state.'

"He was calm. Motionless. Impassive. Playing the honourable death of the Roman. So let him die with conceit. What did I care. And that screaming woman. Throwing her arms around him, jumping up and down, shouting, crying...

"'No. No. You mustn't.' Hysterical.

"'Get out of the way.'"

Even the food on the tray, there's something different today. He's too attentive, not really listening, only pretending to hear. Wants me to believe he's listening to my history, but no, it's my present he wants to know. The telephone. Those questions about calls. What does he care? Has he been listening? Why? What does he know? Has he seen me go out? I can't trust him. A traitor. A potential tyrant.

"'Get out of the way.' I raised my machine-gun. Claretta throwing herself between the gun and his body. Squeezing the trigger. Jammed. Squeezing again. Banging it with my hand. The horrible feeling of nothing.

"His eyes softening. And Claretta in screaming hysterics. I take out my hand gun."

In the park. Has he seen me with Hinckley? For the last months he's been at my door listening to the phone calls. Last night. He knows.

"Rushing at my gun. She screams: 'You can't kill us like this.'

"My hand gun jams. The sweat dripping down my face.

"'Moretti. Your gun, give me your gun.'

"The last scene of the last act, putting on a show right to the end — Mussolini ripping open his jacket, baring his hairy barrel chest, facing me with his jaw, square — 'Shoot me in the chest.'

"Claretta fell first in the spray of bullets from my machine-gun."

I let him know too much — talking to him every day. Who

knows me better than he does? Trusting. And who is he but a spy, a traitor.

"Mussolini was also hit. He almost had time to see Claretta fall to the ground, die quietly as he stumbles back against the wall, slides slowly to the ground, crumbling, legs under his body. Breathing heavily — not dead yet. I walk up. Stand over his body. Empty a round into his chest. His mouth twists in one of his cynical smiles.

"His final expression suits him.

"No one spoke."

◆◆◆

I had to get out. No other choice. They were there waiting for me. I looked through the peep hole in the door and they were in the hall, knocking, trying the door. Both tall, dressed in almost identical brown and grey suits. One slightly overweight, balding, bird eyes darting nervously in every direction. The other with greased down black hair, firm steady eyes and a small neatly trimmed black moustache. I wouldn't answer. Hardly breathing. They went away, looking for me on the beach. No time. A small bag already packed, for two years sitting ready. Taking the stairs, thirteen floors, it never was a lucky number. Leaving from the back door behind the building. If only there's a taxi. To the airport at Faro.

What a shame. It was so comfortable, the room, the beach,

the sun, enjoying life. Why did they have to find me? But I knew it was only a matter of time.

I have to wait an hour for the plane, but they will still be looking for me on the beach, trying the door. It will be hours before they pick the lock. Only the two of them, not another at the airport. To Lisbon. Trying to leave a trail they won't be able to follow. Taking a taxi into the city.

"Would you like to buy some hashish? Would you like to buy a gold watch?"

An old man on crutches falls in front of me. An old woman balancing a bundle on her head turns to look at me. Why, what does she see? Her bundle falls into the street and is instantly hit by a car. These are not signs of welcome, I take a taxi back to the airport.

Hours of waiting — they are so slow. What if the two men following me accidently try Lisbon and find me sitting in this waiting room?

Madrid.

There's an air bridge to Barcelona, a plane every hour. Just missed one. Wait an hour before they announce the flight might be delayed an hour. Another hour. Another hour. There is an unofficial strike; they announce the plane has connection problems and then technical problems. At midnight the union finally frees me.

Barcelona. Into the city by taxi. The Ramblas, the skin district, seedy screaming men, the smell of old urine, gaudy lights, old whores, a cheap hotel. The room has four single beds, a minor dormatory. Dingy, the smell of dirt, a cave. Stained sink and dull lights. I sit on the edge of the bed in the dark. Spanish conversations on the street. Two a.m. Yes, here they will never find me. The tangle too complex for federal agents to sort through. There are rats living in the walls. After the sun this room is too dark, too close to the grave.

Eight a.m. A taxi to the airport.

London. Gatwick. An express train to Victoria. A taxi to an hotel in Leiceister Square — not one of those horrible bed and breakfast pensions crammed with American college students and loud Germans — but a quiet small hotel in the centre of the tourist area. Hidden with the hoards. One more anonymous old tourist. Safe. One hundred metres from ten cinemas, two blocks from as many theatres and twice as many restaurants. Right in the centre.

It is a room again. One firm bed, colour TV, a framed Picasso blue period print hung on a wall covered by plastic imitation linen wall paper. My private toilet with bath and sink in an adjoining carpeted room. Very nice. Complete with kettle, tea pot, cup, saucer, and complimentary tea bags and artificial cream. How English. Yes, this will do nicely.

The TV comes with a Teletext system. I turn it on and read the news. I'm not mentioned. Hinckley isn't mentioned. Our events are forgotten, relegated to history's collective memory outside today's news.

ROBBERY: POLICE HUNT ARMED RAIDERS.

GCHQ: GOVERNMENT CHALLENGES RULING.

DOCKS: UNION AT PEACE TALKS.

PIT ARRESTS AS PICKETING STEPPED UP.

TESTING TIME FOR NUCLEAR RAIL FLASK.

SEARCH RESUMES OVER BODY IN WOOD.

NEW ZEALAND TO DEVALUE DOLLAR.

✦✦✦

The walls are crawling closer. The ceiling collapsing. The insistent rattling of the windows in the wind. The explosive dripping of a faucet. The clock, it's rhythmic ticking, I try not to listen, covering my head with the pillow. Closing my eyes, pressing my face against the sheets, the glaring light stronger than the sun. I throw off the cover and pace the room. Place the clock in a drawer under a thick covering of clothing. Grab the top handle in both hands and try to wrench the drawer closed. I am strangled, choked by the room. The walls, the floor, the ceiling, closing, hands covering my mouth, gripping my throat. My head a hollow drum on which a fist is beating.

He wasn't difficult to capture. The Allies merely had to knock on his door and he answered. He had no image of himself as a criminal and therefore had no need to run or hide. On the contrary, when the Allied military police arrived his initial thoughts were they wanted to take him back to the United States to give President Truman the benefit of his intimate knowledge of conditions in Italy and Japan. Pound was somewhat surprised when he was handcuffed and instead of being put on a plane for the USA was taken by jeep to an American military prison in Pisa.

On these impossible nights I remember Pound's description: the sensation that the top of his head was empty and that his eyebrows were constantly taut in a raised position due to the heat and glare.

They called it the "arse hole of the army." Pound was placed in solitary confinement immediately after his arrest and held incommunicado. Here 3,600 "trainees" were under sentence, five years to life, for their crimes: AWOL, desertion, theft, rape and murder. Here the American government in a display of mercy was allowing them to work out their sentence in one terrible year of fourteen hours of drill per day and close order punishment by night, after which they might be allowed the privilege of re-entering the army.

There was one row of cages in which long-term offenders were confined. The men in the cages were incorrigibles. Pound's cage had been specially built — solid enough to hold the most dangerous beast. Heavy air-strip was welded over galvanized mesh, six by six feet and six and a half feet tall. A tough customer.

It was mid summer. The Italian sun beat down with relentless intensity on the prison yard. The other prisoners were supplied with tents to keep off the heat and glare of the sun, Pound was given no protection so the guards could watch him at all times. A military highway ran nearby. Dust floated everywhere. Food by the time it reached his cage was covered in dust. While others were penned in groups, he was alone in his cage. While other prisoners were let out of their cages for meals and exercise, Pound was always confined. By day he walked in the cage, two paces, two paces, slouched under the tropical sun. The dust. By night a special reflector poured light on his cage alone. Tried to hide, to protect his bloodshot eyes, he kept his head under the blanket.

Everyone, including the incorrigibles, had orders not to speak to him. But Pound spoke. He sat stroking his beard, talking, as the sentry paced and pivoted, paced and pivoted, talking.

After a drenching rain they came to see how he had survived and opened the door wide enough to insert a military cot. This kept him off the concrete but took up space. More rain. A pup tent thrown into the cage. Every evening he would put it up, constantly experimenting with varying constructions, and every morning take it down.

He had one book, a Chinese text of Confucious and a Chinese Dictionary. He spent his time translating.

After three weeks he collapsed. Claustrophobia, partial amnesia, bouts of hysteria and terror. They moved him to a tent in the Medical Compound. He lay on his back, absent and present, singing, "O sweet and lovely, O lady be good."

THE IRONY

Ugly news. Massacre at McDonald's. A man goes berserk with shotgun, rifle and hand gun, killing twenty-two; shooting children, women, anyone who moved and the wounded who moaned. Used metal penetrating bullets. A Vietnam Vet. The largest massacre in US history. An insane man, no intelligence to the act, no premeditation, no purpose, just an ugly moment in history. Instantly I want to forget his name and the stupidity of his actions. But at the same time here is the portrayal of complete cultural desperation. A forty-year-old man, fired from his job — a security man. Likes guns. Argues with his wife. Tries to find her at McDonald's and in the epicenter of junk, kitsch America becomes a human bomb wreaking illogical, random and violent death. The executioner of all those who eat at McDonald's. "I've killed a thousand and I will kill a thousand more." Trained by his country to kill for his country he kills his country. And a police sharpshooter through the window, one bullet in the heart, killed by his country.

An accident in history. A bloody plane crash, a volcano erupting, a moment manifesting a cultural error, a destroyed man.

◆◆◆

The distance is dominated by sounds, machines demanding an acknowledgement of presence, the web of voices audible en masse with the occasional shout distinguishable as a precise word. The horns, always the horns and sirens. Noise, collectively called central London during a summer evening. Differing from Rome or New York or Milan only in the language of the indistinguishable voices. I could open the curtains, stare out the window to give the sounds the tangibility of sight, but that would be to fix the location, to be forced by sight to admit, yes, here in this specific room, at this particular time. But it is my turn to be on watch. We have not eaten in days. Our clothing as much dirt as fabric, our boots held together by rope and dried mud. A real bed and clean sheets the simplicity of our dreams. But no one complains. And if I may speak for the group, no one minds these difficult conditions. We have a purpose.

And when I ask, there is no possible answer, here the absence — the simple purpose. The perseverance of days, the old man's obstinance in the accumulation of time, I can not call it sufficient.

For the past fifteen months we have been fighting

underground. Attacking and retreating. Hitting and hiding.
Always in fear that the army will discover our position, never
sure who is still loyal to the fascist leaders and who are the
partisans. There are four of us left in this cell. Never have
there been more than six — membership is a temporary state.
Death common. Last night Deviro stumbled while planting an
explosive under a retreating German armoured truck. Before
he could scream, disappearing in the blast. The truck was
empty. It was a waste. Unnecessary. The Germans are
retreating. Defeated. Deviro's was an act of vengeance; he
wanted to strike back at the fascists one more time before it
was too late. He is a victim of his own obsession.

It is as though I have fallen victim to the bourgeois state
of fulfillment. Here in this hotel room the demands of the
body are well met: bed and food abundantly supplied without
making any strains on my stockpiled wealth. Entertainment is
provided by the television, by the theatres, the cinemas, the
museums, the walks. I am satisfied with my own
companionship, preferring the solitude to the demands of
another's intrusion. In total, I am content. But it is a stale
tranquillity.

We have one purpose. We are now all agreed. We will find
Mussolini. There will be no divergence from our course with
any undirected acts of violence. Deviro's death, its waste,
stands as a solid reminder.

I sit on the ground, raised slightly from the damp earth by
a few flat stones, leaning against an old stone fence probably
first built by the Romans. There are only minor night sounds.
I am very tired. To walk sixty or eighty kilometres in one day

and then spend the evening on watch is difficult. The others are almost asleep. Their yawns contagious.

How many soldiers in the last five years have rested in this abandoned building. Broken bottles, rusted tin cans, cigarette butts and empty shells. This wall smells of death. Who did the fascists execute here? It was not recent, there are no traces of blood. But blood disappears so slowly. The lightest rain may cleanse the ground but not the memory.

♦♦♦

I have no urge to participate in the sights of London. I seldom walk the streets — too many bodies forcing me against walls, posts, pushing me into traffic. The cabs here are vicious — the less agile are in constant jeopardy. No, I am back in the room. I tried watching television but it is completely boring.

I sit here listening to the street. Not listening, just sitting. No longer do I have a purpose. But I am still alive and nervous. Not afraid they will find me, but nervous.

The time on the beach, in the small apartment in Portugal, it was possible to rest. I had just failed and needed a period of death. This escape has forced me again to wake. Nervously I rub my forehead, pass my fingers through the remains of my hair.

And I must.

Sitting here in this hotel room, this small room in Leiceister Square above an expensive seafood restaurant. How many rooms are there in which I have sat alone? How many before me have sat in their rooms? History is filled with my counterparts. How many are sitting alone in their rooms at this very instant? Not my concern; I only know this room.

Once more before I die. But enough of the past; I am tired of being a judge and executioner.

I don't want to lie down and die. But not to be destructive. So difficult. There is nothing outside the window but traffic — the movement of machines and bodies — passing.

◆◆◆

It is inside the small location where I am able to understand, to at least for the moment be allowed a luxury, the feeling of comprehension. It has always been this limited loci. Against the immensity of history it was in my moment, in the time it took for the first bullet to leave the gun's muzzle and enter Mussolini's chest, that I felt secure in the knowledge of my own existence. All previous events were a wave leading to this precise moment. History pushed me forward to the moment of Mussolini's death so I could be given life in history. But it was such a fixed instant; again, merely the time of the bullet from the gun to his body. I have been abandoned. As though that wave on which I rode reached shore to dissolve, not to return to the sea for re-formation and re-emergence, as though once washed ashore here was my place, to remain in the quietude of memory forever, never to re-emerge from the confines of this my single historical moment. When I entered the room in Toronto I wasn't intending to open the door again except to receive food. Hinckley was an error. It was his moment in history I was aiding in creating, not mine, yet his lack of success was my failure.

The retreats, the escapes leading to this hotel room were the consequence of the few centimetres right or left of the bullet's entry, the difference between death and life, success or failure. And therefore, in the confines of this room I am held in a fading history deprived of a future destiny. What is this word destiny? It feels so ancient, borrowed from Greek tragedy. And possibly, if I was presumptuous, it would be, but the situation is not so much tragic as commonplace, tragic in its mundanity, the situation of the common human condition. Here in the panoramic view of the landscape of history I am almost imperceptible. It is that microscopic, sub-particle "almost" which is my room, this hotel room with its single bed, single washbasin, single table, chair and window. This introspective room lost in memory is also this "almost."

As long as I am without action, preoccupied only with the twin diseases of introspection and memory, the panorama continues to expand, my room, my moment, my "almost" diminishes, being perpetually absorbed in the ever increasing distance. When the child asks: "Who was Mussolini?" I am still alive, but for how long will this fragile edifice continue to hold? The justness of my action, that Mussolini deserved to die untried at the hands of a partisan, that I was merely an instrument of justice and not an illogical assassin only makes my position more vulnerable, in the panoramic distance I am half concealed in a shadow.

History set the trap in which I have been caught and held. This beneign jailor tended my bodily needs in his ever-tightening room, permitting innumerable outings in the free access of memory. But it is only a ploy, an illusionary freedom, an old man's cane designed to carry him from sleep back to sleep.

An evening with too much light, a dangerous cloudless moon capable of turning a man into a target at one hundred metres. A night fit to discover a new menace. With the increased German presence in the area our lives didn't need the challenge of an additional enemy.

The thick woods and the shadow of a rock face provided a relatively comfortable and safe locale for our small smokeless fire. The coffee and the plan for tomorrow's raid both making progress when the sound of gun fire and explosions sent us scrambling for our rifles and cover. It was near, too near. Not more than five or six hundred metres. It became evident that we were not under attack as the firing continued, erratic, not advancing on our position. Extinguishing the fire, cautiously creeping toward the sound — perhaps to discover a fellow band of partisans under German attack — hoping to provide aid by positioning ourselves at the enemy's unguarded rear.

From a vantage point of 150 metres, an unexpected apparition, a group of nine or ten boys, armed with hand guns, rifles and bottles, drinking, firing at trees, into the air, at the emptied bottles. There was something ugly, sinister about this party of boys, not yet men, playing with guns and alcohol. Each dressed in a freshly laundered or a new black shirt. We kept to our hidden positions observing this unfriendly party.

This ugly sighting wasn't explained until three days later when Petro returned from a neighbouring farm with supplies and news. An Italian SS had been formed. Recruits were taken from the boy's reformatory in Florence by selecting the most incorrigible, violent, meanest and stupidest members of a generally unruly lot — the worst of the worst boys. We had witnessed a spontaneous practice session of this neophite Italian SS which had already distinguished itself by numerous arrests — some on the charge of giving assistance to British prisoners, but most merely on vague unspecified charges. The feeling throughout the countryside surrounding Florence is that no anti-fascist is safe. The arrests generally take place in the early morning, when the victims are in bed, and their families are left in complete ignorance of where they have been taken. The questioning is often brutal and prolonged — sometimes they are mysteriously released or they disappear completely. They have succeeded in producing an uneasiness throughout the area; Petro was greeted with a great deal of suspicion.

These are mindless, vicious animals. If we had known that initial evening what we learned later, we would have opened fire and exterminated the larva in its incubation.

◆◆◆

Always dressed in military fatigues. The dark glasses of

the dictator, but a man who says he wants to relinquish his power, who wants to serve, not lead. I watch this dreamer of revolutions, not the administrator of everyday power, on television. His Russian AK-47 rifle leaning against the administrative desk, not the military dictator, but a worker for the new order. Jerry Rawlings tells me:

> *The political, judicial and legislative institutions were the legacies of colonialism, designed to perpetuate the rule of a privileged elite serving the economic interests of the developed countries. It is very questionable whether, even with fairly radical reforms, such institutions can form the basis of stable representative government relevant to the majority of the people.*

> *Truly participatory democracy needs new structures which will gradually provide the means of involving the people.*

> *Revolution means transformation. No trans-formation of a society can be immediate, except in fairy tales. While gradually dismantling structure s which are irrelevant to our situation, we are building new ones.*

> *It was not I who had lost confidence. The system had failed again and again. For the masses it was a meaningless procedure, allowing no participation*

other than putting a piece of paper into a box once
every few years. It was clear that without structural
changes there can be no transformation of society.

◆◆◆

A yawn: one of those days when the mouth persists in gaping, opening, the brain refuses to work. I could blame it on age, call it creeping senility, but the condition is much more prevalent than just today. Years of yawns.

Just to lie down and sleep, that would be the solution. To give into the drowsiness. But I have a job to do. I can't sleep. But there is no one here watching. Who would know. Who would care?

◆◆◆

She bends down and picks up the magazine which has fallen from my jacket pocket. I've seen her: sitting by herself in this restaurant, writing. "Do you mind if I look at it for a moment?"

"No. Not at all." A moment. Who is this woman? What does she want with my copy of a third world news magazine? I drink my tea. The waitress asks me if I would like another cup. "Yes."

142

✦✦✦

Without anyone's presence edifices crumble. Rock is washed by sea. Uninhabited buildings slide from sight back into the ground. The activity does not cease. There is no quietude, only imaginary moments of rest. Replacement is perpetual. I sat by the window and thought of the snow melting from the branches of a tree. It was so long ago.

✦✦✦

"Do you mind if I join you?" Sitting across from me at a small restaurant table. "I'll have another coffee — please — would you like something else?— for myself, a chocolate donut."

"An order of unbuttered toast. Please."

The waitress scratches her note pad with a greasy pencil. Leaves.

This young woman sitting, the copy of the magazine between us.

"I'm a student. Reading history."

✦✦✦

It is not the past which has been constantly present, sitting perpetually beside me with the confidence of a religious man, but the absence of the future. A shift, a change, a release from the grasp of my constant companion in solitude, my past, my moment in history: "I'm a student. Reading history."

It is this fixation with the past which acted as my ground strength, perhaps which allowed me a voice to hear, an ear, a response in my solitude. But now when I look at this girl, I realize the absence of speech, of my speech and of my listening to the speech of others. Has it been years? How many thousands of meals have I eaten in silence? It is with difficulty, almost as a test, I begin again the simplest of articulations: "I thought I told the waitress, no butter."

And the girl responds, "You did. It is kind of greasy, isn't it." This banal, stilted exchange is the beginning of conversation. She is no longer an intrusion. I begin to see her — as she congeals from shadow to substance. She is not very old, or very young, perhaps in her mid-twenties. Dark, with black straight hair and the hint of a moustache on her upper lip. Thin, to the point of illness. But what dominates is a nervousness, a constant movement of her body, a hyperactivity. Her lips are in constant motion yet emit no sound. She carries on an inaudible monologue. I strain, listening, yet hear no sound — or perhaps the words are too loud, too high pitched, beyond the capacity of my hearing. The quivering of the lips, the darting of the eyes, the mouth beginning to form a smile then suddenly straightening: a face never at rest.

I've finished my toast and tea and she has taken one small

bite from her chocolate donut — from the covering — picking
at it with her fingers as she talks and says nothing.

Her eyes move nervously from the ceiling to the floor,
from her lap to a point behind my head. Yet the superficial
feeling is of stillness. The look is bewilderment. Mouth half
open. Fumbling in her bag to produce a package of cigarettes.
Shaking her head negatively: "No. No. Should I. Do you mind
if I smoke? I've been trying to stop. Would you like one?"

I almost reach out to accept, but draw back, slowly,
shaking my head in response. Soon.

Her mouth, her lips moving, except now I can hear her
and she is sitting behind a dense covering of smoke produced
by rapid inhales and exhales of her cigarette. She smokes with
a vengeance, trying to rid herself of the cigarette as quickly as
possible.

The waitress throwing down the bill on the table does so
with more than her usual disdain. I have the distinct feeling
that she finds something wrong with both of us.

"No. Just another tea would be fine."

◆◆◆

Yesterday in the restaurant — am I supposed to
understand? We talked for the entire afternoon. I don't
remember anything she said, or I said. I think we both talked
incessantly without ever listening to each other. It was
enjoyable once again to create myself for an other. What we

have in common is an individual interest in ourselves and in history — which makes us instantly close. To create a tangible token of need to meet, she borrowed my magazine and will return it tomorrow at noon.

There is a potential here. The form is not clear. There is obviously no other choice for either of us.

Yes.

We must learn how to talk to each other. She has to listen and hear what I say.

◆◆◆

The waitress has categorized me: a silent, solitary old man who occupies a table near the restaurant's south window, orders little, sits for extended periods staring into the street, and tips slightly above average. She is angry or at least destabilized that I, whose name in three years of almost daily visits she never inquired after, have dared to break the routine. She fails to understand: this is not a routine, merely the chance repetition of similar movements. Every day I enter the restaurant it is without intent, never have I set out to have tea in this particular locale, it is merely conveniently located at a distance not too far, nor too near my hotel room, and the choice of a seat by the south window is one of vantage, providing me with the entertainment of the street; and as for ordering tea and toast, it is merely what I feel like eating at that time of day. She is wrong, I am not a man of habit, it is preference, I am a man who prefers this particular restaurant, this table, this view and this food.

The girl arrived late. During the tenure of my expectancy the waitress appeared to be gloating, assured that the world had again returned to its proper order. And now she is standing over us, defiant, one hand on her hip, pen raised, arrogantly daring us to commit further indiscretions in her presence. When I order a cheese sandwich, I think for an instant she will refuse my order, but the normal routine is reestablished when I order tea and the girl buttered toast. The waitress might have been smiling when she returned with our order.

◆◆◆

By the second week of daily meetings our presence is accepted — the waitress, the girl and myself have arrived at an equilibrium: we all three belong at this restaurant, two of us at this table sitting, eating, drinking, talking, and one of us standing. The girl no longer appears to be moving her lips and emitting silence. The general tremor of her body has diminished. Nothing as radical as a quietude, but rather in possession of a direction for the nervousness, the conversation a channel for her pent-up energy. And yes, I too, but on the other extreme, in abandoning my solitude have also abandoned my lethargy. As though the girl and I have reached a state of balance, absorbing each other's extremes to arrive at the equilibrium of conversation.

✦✦✦

"I read the articles. Of course. But... I think she wants to take your order. No, I'll just have a coffee. The approach is still too concerned with capitalist economic concerns. The description of Bhindranwale's death struggle in the Golden Temple does display Gandhi's tyrannical nature. No. I wanted a coffee not a tea. Milk. I wish the followers of a religion would stop and think once in a while. Who needs it.

"And the article on Ghana. Especially on... on... what's his name...?"

"Jerry Rawlings."

"Flight-Lieutenant Jerry Rawlings. I want to know more.

"But those parts of the article when the writer intimates that he's a potential dictator. And its problematic, the fact, twice acting with military force to discontinue democratic rule."

"But he said it himself: 'What form of democracy is it that is nothing more than placing a marked piece of paper in a box every three or four years?'"

"But does he try to give the people more power? I realize that voting is a façade, but it is a basic, an unequivocable element of the social contract. Rawlings is correct that the mode of voting is inadequate, but energy should be spent in trying to expand the base of power not transferring it into the hands of unelected representatives."

✦✦✦

Here, through this girl reading history at Oxford I am being transformed into a student. A freshman engaged in emotional political discussion. This restaurant our common room, our texts articles from third world newsmagazines. The half-century difference in our experiences is vaporizing in the commonalty of a mutual desire. But what is this desire? It is more than a longing for the acquisition of information, or an understanding of history, neither the present or the past. Future. And only future.

◆◆◆

"The two elderly women in the corner table sipping their tea, slowly chewing their buttered muffins, what is their will — for the future: 'Oh dear, our pension cheques, I hope no one was hurt.' The family by the window, house mother, office father, two school children, the waitress impatiently waiting for their orders, no we don't have half portions, Kevin stop squirming, what would they say to a military coup? 'Impossible. It wasn't that bad. What's going to happen to business?' No, a military take over of power within the democratic first world is unthinkable, a regression. The structures have been established which guarantee basic freedom and comfort. Improvements are certainly necessary and important, but, the expenditure of energy should be toward a broadened democracy where individuals are allowed more say not less."

"A common working together. But people are basically lazy."

"No they're not. Give them a feeling of spirit, a desire to want improvement, a better way and..."

"They will take the easy way out, saying, 'It's not so bad, I could make it better, but it's just too much work.'"

"But without increased individual effort you have totalitarianism. Do you actually think people like to be told what to do?"

"Some people. There are a limited number of leaders and an infinite number of followers."

"It's so confusing. I can hold it for a little while, then I lose it. Sliding from my thinking. I can feel it fading. Too much to take into account."

"That's when you decide to act. All the thoughts spontaneously materializing as an action which represents all your conscious and unconscious thinking — equal to and better than all your thoughts."

◆◆◆

I have heard some speak as though they had a positive or even a constructive relationship with time, as though an understanding had been struck, as though they had traded part of themselves and in return, time had granted them some small part of itself. These are the same individuals whom I see at historic sites congratulating themselves before a fallen pillar, but for what, that after 3,000 years there still remains a pillar, a past, a ruin, a fragment. Or are they congratulating themselves on their superiority, that 3,000 years after the fact they are alive to stand here admiring the past? I don't understand those who have made even a loose bargain with time. They built themselves an edifice which they call time. I have no trust in this edifice — at a distance it may be admirable but it is merely a façade. These are the same people who feel comfortable with earth, admiring its potential for regeneration. In earth I see only the place of my death, the vanishing of my body. I don't hold my grandmother in this piece of mud. Those who stare at the sea and behold the immensity of time and feel a certain quietude are either fools or deluded optimists. Below sea and earth there is only absence, not life. Hell is not situated in the sky but in the bowels of the earth. Time is not a sunrise but an endless series of sunsets, not light but the absence of light. To be a simpleton is to see eternity in a rock, or life in a grain of sand. I see even the sun as an embodiment of death. Every breath we take is always our last. It is all disappearance. No, I'm not being pessimistic nor obstinate. These are not the mutterings of an old senile man, but the bare truth, reality. Any other articulation of the situation is a lie. Let this stand as the truth — time is not two edged — it is not the sword of salvation and damnation: it has never been defeated. Look among the grains of sand on the beach and you will find the disintegrated remains of bones. And the sound of the sea will be silence. Ask the old man, he knows.

✦✦✦

Sitting, not speaking, not looking at anything in particular he is a man occupied. As though a man, who having acquired too many centimetres of waistline has imposed a strict diet upon himself, and now sits, hungry, quietly waiting for the fat to dissolve, by an act of will attempting to restore a former physique.

A series of coincidences — the same: restaurant; day; time of day; a similar taste in choice of table looking out onto the street; a fallen magazine. These causes on their own would not have been enough. For me, it was the absence, particularly the eyes. Not here, but not emptiness, the gaze located, but not in this restaurant. And when I sat down as though I had been expected, the resumption of a long acquaintance; I was returning after a short absence.

✦✦✦

Politics. Constantly turning the conversation back to this one interest. But it is a politics devoid of history, of any mention of a past, centred always on the present of today's newscast, today's newspaper. We sit in the restaurant discussing the details and ramifications of this day's particular news: tomorrow, today will have vaporized, be forgotten. If I refer to yesterday's event today, or today's event tomorrow, there will be no response. He obviously hears me — his silence is evidence enough. If I persist, try to draw yesterday into the logical continuum of today, his silence becomes more persistent, his eyes become darker turning from brown to black, until they have disappeared, and I am alone.

It is as though he is attempting to solve a difficult problem. The state of his progress: basic, the first stage has not been completed, he has not yet succeeded in formulating the question. He is actively involved in discovering the problem he knows demands a solution.

◆◆◆

She examines me, what else could she be doing, staring, her bottom lip beginning to quiver, the upper lip already in motion. On the edge of speech, yet no sound. Examining. Talking to herself about me. And before she can burden me with analysis, or worse, a question, I ask:

"And, what is it we should be doing?"

"Does there, is it necessary, we should be involved in an action, doing something as you describe it?"

This is no answer. We have discussed this before, the necessity, the undisputable necessity of...

"An action." She is beginning to understand.

Asks: "One action?"

"Something visible."

"Visible? To whom?"

"History?"

She is leaning forward. Of course, nervously waiting for my pronouncement. But there is nothing. Here is the barrier. There is nothing."

"An action. An action."

Silence. Sliding back into our chairs. Her mouth slightly open. I take a sip of tea — it's cold, the milk has congealed on the surface.

"But what?"

"It'll come."

"You realize we are involved in a trap?"

"Yes."

"History."

"Sure."

✦✦✦

It was decided: we would do something together. The old assassin and the student. But what and where? Could we do it in England, in London, it didn't seem possible. So confined. Restricted. Developed. An old world fixed in its ways. The economy could be considered bad, unemployment high, but it wasn't all bad, new hamburger restaurants were opening every day. No one was starving on the street. Violence was low. Too secure, too developed a country. Not here.

"The Third World."

And we spent the afternoon together in the famous

London reading room — probably at the same table where Marx had sat a hundred years before, researching, writing, critiquing — trying to find the right country for our intervention.

◆◆◆

He intimates there is a large sum, a treasure he calls it, to aid our project — but what project? A fantasy developed by an old man as a crutch to see himself through the difficult diminishing years. The money and the project are the fabrications of sustenance. I empathize. After the excitement of my first year at Oxford, when the door was held open for my entry and I literally bounded with exuberance and energy, eager to begin my dance with knowledge, my wedding with history. Halfway through my second year the romance turned to drudgery. History revealed itself as an old woman with bad breath. My initial questions forgotten.

This old man who holds his tea cup at a discreet distance before tilting it gracefully to his lips, this man whose English often collapses into an indecipherable mixture of Italian and English silences, whose eyes disappear to black and return glowing, is himself an embodiment of history, possessing more of that which initially excited me than twenty of those Oxford men of learning in their black robes and flat hats — better costumes for sleeping than learning — and their pompous lectures and elaborate footnotes and bibliographic references. This old man who refuses to speak of the past, whose only interest is an impossible plan he can't formulate, is my history lesson. I have no evidence to substantiate this hypothesis, no proper argument or accepted methodology, but if the university had any sophistication I would be permitted to present this man as my final thesis. Yes, here, look at him, ask him to drink a cup of tea, watch his eyes, listen to his desire to act, to his confusion, to his silence and you will have history. And this is why I am drawn back, day after day to this restaurant, this table, to this doddering old man, why I have refused to return to the propricty of Oxford and to the correct books on the necessary topics. I haven't told him of my reasons, of my life, he doesn't ask. Either he understands or it isn't necessary, but necessary for what? His project? But possibly, yes possibly there is something to his insistence that he will direct his secret wealth to this project, this fantasy future which can be solved by one well directed action. An old romantic humanitarian — one of the last of his kind still alive in the final days of the twentieth century. Yes, we are similar. It is more than mere empathy which draws me. As though he is my return, the life I first desired for history and lost.

◆◆◆

I don't feel well today. Barely enough energy to raise my head from the pillow. I have to get out of bed. Noon. Told her we'd meet in the restaurant. But I just want to sleep. There is no pain only a fog, a drowsiness. Close my eyes. Sleep returns. I want to meet her. Three weeks of meeting, and it has become a custom. Every day we begin at noon and sit for three, four hours ordering tea, toast and sometimes soup. Our plans are growing steadily, but not today. I close my eyes and the world continues to spin. Nothing I can do but attempt to ride out the winds of my body, hope that I have the strength to hold until the evening and then hope for a better tomorrow. It has been occurring more often, this distancing, this absence, this mist inside my body. Not daily yet, that would be death, the end.

At first it was only occasional, waking after an uneasy night, half rested, more exhausted than when I went to bed. The first time it was frightening. The exhaustion was total, the entire day had to be spent either sleeping or lying in bed. After it occurred a few times the fear dissipated but the discomfort, the irritation at the inability to function was frustrating. Now this state of forced convalescence occurs at least once a week and sometimes two attacks are barely separated by two days of active grace. She will understand; I've warned her. During our first weeks of meetings I was free of attacks, every day free of the oppression, a blessing, a welcome surprise. She will wait drinking coffee by herself and tomorrow return for our meeting. We are both waiting for each other, an unequivocal need which cannot be erased by the absence of just one day. I close my eyes and float in an emptiness, in an absence. Not the pleasure of rest but an obvious training, a trial run. I must hurry. Sleeping uncomfortably.

◆◆◆

Directly behind her, I can't help but watch, an obese man consuming his second plate of food; his mouth is in constant motion, his fork a mechanical device between plate and mouth, plate and mouth. He reminds me of someone. I am avoiding her eyes. We are having our first argument not about political theory. She is sitting in an unaccustomed fashion, silent. The trembling of her lips, intense, so rapid they appear still. A dangerous situation. Not one word. The man has just ordered more food. Hinckley, he reminds me of Hinckley. She has made basically a harmless request; I suppose merely curiosity. Why do I insist on maintaining my privacy? What is there to hide? What difference should it make to have her visit my room, no secret documents, no cache of dangerous weapons. Only a small room. The waitress has brought him a large piece of apple pie with two mounds of ice cream dripping over the sides of the crust. I steal a look, she is watching me, waiting for a response.

Why is she insisting on entering? How many years has it been since I opened the door and invited someone into my privacy? My privacy. What does she want inside my room which can't be obtained in the restaurant? We talk, exchange looks, eat, and plan: what more can we do in the room? She has already invaded my life and I welcomed the occupation. What symbolic gesture do I intuitively interpret from her request? A presence in a larger part of my physical situation, another part of myself? Why am I frightened, trying to hold a small secret of myself within this locked room? And what would she discover on entering? Nothing, a rented hotel room, almost totally devoid of my personality, nothing more than rented walls and rented furniture, a locale where the anonymous pass the night and then depart. The obese man is leaving, belching loudly as he passes our table, an acknowledgement of my voyeurism during his meal, sharing this last mark of pleasure with his uninvited guest. She pretends not to notice.

Solitude, jealously protecting its territory. We are arguing in silence. Not the harsh exchange of cutting words but the penetrating blows of silence. The stirring of my cold tea is a deafening disturbance, a display of my weakening position. The silent picking at her bran muffin, threatening her mouth with the food, teasing herself, restraining from eating until the muffin is a line of crumbs on the table, is a sign of her gain, her ascendancy in the argument.

The waitress reading the tension at our table maintains her distance. Today is devoid of elaborate plans of action, of future potential, the mountain is visibly eroding.

◆◆◆

The fickle collective unconscious is really an occasionally awakened unconsciousness. Living for most is a thick blanket of events punctuated with the unexpected flash, an interrupted blackness under which we doze. Do you remember such and such? Who? Yes, oh him, I remember, just forgot his name. What was he supposed to have done? Didn't he die violently? They ran his car off the road at night, made it look like an accident. At his funeral all of Athens, all of Greece from Macedonia to the Aegean Islands, took to the streets, sweeping the air with a relentless, obsessive roar of grief: "He lives, he lives, he lives." And he did live for that day in Athens in the hearts of two million, the people, the streets mourning the murder of a hero. At the church, beside the grave, the priest dripping gold and precious jewels, chanted: "Eonia imi tou esou. May your memory be eternal." But who is this man that the ruling tyrant ordered murdered? A man who has become part of history, but we do not know his name, if I said Alekos Panagoulis would you shrug your shoulders or nod yes, him? In Greece where he fought and died they might remember but not here. History prefers to stay at home, holding firmly to the ground on which it occurred. A local hero for a small town.

Here was a man who attempted to kill a tyrant and failed. The bomb under George Papadopoulos' car barely damaged the automobile. What had failed? The charge? The timing? The executioner had pushed the plunger a third of a second too late — the intervention of fate, of chance. The tyrant lived to capture and torture the man, and eventually make him a hero, a martyr. But when the tyrant was finally defeated and power supposedly returned to the people, the hero's actions no longer needed to be remembered. While the tyrant remained there was a need to remember, but with his defeat there was a need to begin forgetting. In the future when another tyrant is strangling the people, a name will suddenly be remembered, the martyr will again be necessary, his actions resurrected for inspiration. But he failed to kill the man, is this what they will remember, or will it be the memory of the hero's death for opposing the tyrant with a proud arrogance and tenacity? In another city, in another country men like ourselves will always be remembered at the appropriate time. As we were allowed our few first moments, so after our deaths, we might again be allowed a brief moment in future's memory.

◆◆◆

At first she merely visited.

Insisting that we have a pot of tea in my room — plugging in the kettle, pouring, handing me the cup, adding my cream. Passively I sit on the edge of the bed watching. She turns on the television, plays with the remote channel changer, trying every station, turning it off, turning it on, trying the teletext, super-imposing the text over every channel. Pouring more tea. All without either of us speaking a word. Not communicating with each other. Both in the same room, both alone. Occupying the confines of the same four walls, but each of us occupying a different room.

When the tea is complete and the television has become a bore, she takes a book off the bed table, sits in the room's one armchair, reads. I lie on the bed, on my stomach and read a magazine: it all seems natural.

"Do you want to hear something?" I ask her, waving my magazine in the air.

"I guess so," placing the open book on her lap.

"Remember our conversation about Ghana the..."

"You mean Jerry Rawlings."

"There's an article on Joyce Aryee, Secretary for Information of Ghana's Provisional National Defense Council."

She is sitting attentive, waiting for me to read.

"There appears to be a problem with their revolution. She's been fighting misinformation, trying to explain that: 'Revolutions depend entirely on the social conditions within a country and this means that revolution is not exportable, it is not importable.'"

"Does she think their revolution has taken place in an historical vacuum?"

"I think she's referring more to the entire problem of propaganda being employed by their enemies, actual lies being told, for example: 'That the Cuban troops who will be leaving Angola are coming to Ghana and that fifty of them are already in place.'"

"It's the persistent problem of media distortion."

"The media doesn't distort, it is only a medium, a voice for those supplying the lies."

"And the media in turn becomes a lie and they are the liars."

She is leaning forward in her chair. I am now sitting on the edge of the bed. We are facing each other, beginning an argument, back in the restaurant, the waitress delivering my tea, her <u>coffee</u> during one of our debates.

"It appears that Ghana's neighbours have been less than neutral, aiding those who oppose the revolution."

"Reactionaries!"

"Exactly. Aryee has become almost a romantic, maintaining that Ghana has always played a leadership role in African politics, therefore there is an historical suspicion from her neighbours. Then she admits that Ghana's revolutionary ideas are a threat to the tiny privileged minority who have taken power in many African states and who gain advantage from the neo-imperialist dynamic."

"Does she maintain that their neighbours would rather have oligarchies than democracies?" And I turn the page of the magazine looking for the answer to her question — and there in the second paragraph from the bottom.

"Yes."

The discussion continues till late in the evening. She tries the television. All the channels have signed off, only teletext remains. Shrugs her shoulders, remains. Undresses and gets into bed. Yawns. I undress and get into the other half of the bed. We are lying back to back. It is a double bed but it is now two single beds separated by a wide chasm.

I turn out the light.

The room is filled with the sound of her breathing. I wonder if her room is filled with the sounds of my breathing.

It is only with difficulty that I can recollect the last time I occupied a room with someone else, and it is beyond all hope of recollection when I last shared a bed with another body.

I turn over on my back. Steal a look. She is sleeping — I

think — can't really tell, her back to me, but her breathing has
become slower, deeper.

I don't mind her presence. Seems natural. With the light
from the window I watch her, unabashedly staring at the back
of her neck and its fine black hairs, a number of beauty marks,
three on her shoulders, one left, two right, and one on her
neck. And I pass into sleep staring. During the night, waking,
staring. But in the morning when I get up, the bed is empty.
She is gone. The book has been returned to the night table, the
tea service is clean, in place, and my magazine is face down
on top of the television.

◆◆◆

"Life becomes longer as it grows shorter"; that's what he
told me last night. Watching a rerun of *The Saint*, he waited
for a commercial, then said, or rather pronounced, with the
same rhythm as the announcer proclaiming the benefits of
Palmolive Soap, "Life becomes longer as it grows shorter."
Then he paused, the music rose as a woman splashed
refreshing water on her soap covered face — a dramatic pause
— and asked: "Do you think this is the logic of an old man?"

I pretended to ponder his question with all due
seriousness, a few seconds, trying not to overdo it, and then
merely shook my head negatively, not too vigorously,
returning my attention to the television. He appeared
reassured. But isn't that precisely what it was, the question of

an old man, the logic of an acute mind struggling with a body unable to maintain its half of the bargain. Not that his question was important or profound, it could have been any half-muttered complaint about any topic, asking someone much younger for reassurance. Is this our project, my assignment? He will interrupt a television program, hold out his hand and I will accept it, pat it gently, he will be reassured and I will return to my entertainment and he to his dreams? There was more, this is a lie. He is not reassured. The insincerity in the contrived nod of my head would be detected by this man who believes almost nothing he hears. It is the reverse. I am not the one placating, rather I am being placated. I am not here to help him but to ask for his help. His project may be a fantasy but it is more real than anything else in my life, past or present. My only necessity. With these pronouncements and questions he probes my sincerity. I'm learning. I'll be ready for his next question. Neither of us has time for lies.

✦✦✦

It was almost impossible to get up this morning. My head resting lightly on the pillow. Not that it is painful, this inability to move, not wanting to leave the warm comfortable enclosure of mattress and blankets, rather it is frighteningly easy remaining in bed on the shore of sleep. I am losing my edge, I've noticed myself being mildly pleasant. No longer is it necessary for me to exercise a profound strength of will to be nice. Sleep has become a pleasure not a necessity. Easily the night is the most pleasant part of the day. Am I dying by entropy and enjoying the process?

◆◆◆

I am standing over his bed, pushing at his shoulder, pushing. He opens his eyes, slightly, closes them again.

"It isn't fair. Get up. Get up." He has no right to do this to me. I'm not going to be his nurse. He is trying to desert me. I grab him by the shoulder, clutching the bone and withered muscle, pushing, shouting, "Get up," violently shaking, screaming in desperation.

He's given up. This old man is giving himself up to uselessness, allowing the end to take him quietly in sleep.

"I won't. I won't. What am I supposed to do? Follow your orders? Obey your commands?" I am having trouble controlling my anger. Abandoned. "What are you, some great general directing his campaign from his bed and how do you see me, your faithful adjunct carrying out your well-conceived plans?" I slap him across the face, "No, not for me."

His voice fainter. "You don't understand, we'll make the plans together and ... " I slap him again.

"Forget it." Standing over him. Back and forth hitting him. The palms of my hands against his face, his head wrenched right, and I scream, completely wild, "You're not going to die yet. I won't let you." His eyes wide open. "You have to act."

I'm either going to kill him or beat him back to life. A smile appears on his face, I stop, bend down, my mouth on his ear, whispering, "You're not dead. You can feel it, life." He laughs. It's worked. Quietly, slowly, helping him out of bed into the armchair.

It's alright now, he's back, just a difficult morning, one of those days when it takes longer to rid oneself of the heavy sleep, the drowsiness of a long night. "I was frightened."

With the acknowledgement of blood from the side of his mouth, I am reassured, yes we have a project. For the first time, I kiss him. I lick the blood from the side of his mouth. I can feel him respond, the hardness of his lips thawing. The future will take place.

◆◆◆

"Attempts at dictatorship can exist in every possible guise. The waiter who lords over your table, turning his nose into the air with disgust at the slowness you display in choosing the appetizer. The hotel clerk who offers you the basement room at an exorbitant price. No, the attempts at tyranny are everyday. Not one waking moment transpires when you are not in violation of someone's petty rule, by even your smallest action contravening a code of someone else's design. And the more you laugh at their petty irritations, turn your back on their demands, the greater is their ire, the pitch of their voices, the waving of their hands and arms. And if you persist,

167

consistently and forcefully not to obey, they have been known to arm themselves with clubs and guns, chains and knives and the next time you turn your back in the act of an infraction they will attack with a torrent of malice, brutality and blood. The little dictators need their totalitarian territories to sustain their daily selves. They need your submission on which to exercise their wills. They will always find willing subjects, but with you and I, it is the imperative of our behaviour to act against their tyranny. Witness the smallest manifestation of totalitarianism and it is your responsibility to act."

She listened attentively.

"But..."

"There is always a but."

"Do you believe in tyrannicide?" She asked.

"I used to."

"And now?"

"I'm not so sure."

◆◆◆

It has been decided by a joint evaluation of the situation: whenever possible the room must be abandoned and a regular routine of the restaurant reinstated. The room is entrenched in the possibility of sleep.

It has been at least three months since our last visit to the restaurant. The waitress hasn't forgotten us, it is obvious in the quick turn of her head and the piercing examination over her poised pen — her coffee, my tea, and our single shared order of buttered, white bread toast.

"The possibilities of action seem endless."

Even the waitress's suspicion, her continued lack of trust, offer us a reassuring energy, a conformation of a universal stability from which we may proceed with confidence.

Outside the restaurant a constant stream of traffic. Half the cars are large black taxis, the passengers in the rear seats behind sliding glass partitions, business men hidden in their newspapers, shoppers with their cargo of recent acquisitions, men, women, children, the passengers of our plans.

♦♦♦

It was beginning to rain, umbrellas maliciously appearing, the motion increasing as every possible taxi is solicited and occupied, as the pedestrians hurry across the intersections, dart in and out of the covering of awnings and buildings. Londoners, used to the almost daily occurrence of rain but still, this natural desire to keep oneself dry, to avoid the discomfort.

♦♦♦

"In Upper Volta, I don't understand when they say their revolution isn't exportable. All attempts at revolutionary development are examples. The notion of how to apply the revolutionary concept to your locale must be constantly under consideration."

"Which is precisely our beginning, to decide on the location of our intervention. South America? Central America? Asia? Africa? Which Third World Country will it be?"

"A country in trouble, one suffering famine, a drought. The people starving."

"Or a country under constant attack by their neighbours."

"Why not a country suffering from a plague."

"Which one: disease, war or famine?"

"Why not all of them?"

"Mozambique? Swaziland? Ethiopia?"

"I think we need a map."

◆◆◆

It was more than minor scepticism, more than the appropriate doubt when he told me about the money. I was without belief. Another of his harmless fantasies, another straw at which he was grabbing. And why would I object, if it helped him sustain some purpose in life. It had also become my purpose. I had officially withdrawn from Oxford — history wasn't hiding in the rarefied air of their lecture halls. But yesterday, on the way to the restaurant when we stopped in front of the bank, it all changed. At first I refused to enter, trying, I told myself, to spare him from a very embarrassing scene, but his insistence was impossible to contravene.

He demanded to see the manager, immediately. Not put off by the teller's arrogant quip about an appointment, "The manager is a very busy man."

I kept tugging his arm, "Maybe we should come back tomorrow?" Looking for the door, "We can make an appointment." I was so embarrassed. All the clerks and tellers sending cutting glances: uncouth intruders into their domain. I muttered uselessly, suggesting our immediate retreat.

My first indication of the manager's presence was his firm handshake vibrating through Walter's body to my supporting arm. The manager greeted him by name and lead us cordially down a series of corridors to his private office.

The old man wasn't lying. Cunning, no, he had always told me the truth; it was I who read suspicion into the simple statement of his wealth. He was rich. Not a fantasy, not a ploy: a flat fact, an irrefutable condition. I almost felt cheated of the complexity contained in the possibility that it was a lie. It occurred to me, what else had he told me which was actually true, and I again felt lied to, cheated. I thought I understood, but here in this simple truth everything I doubted was in doubt.

Only later in the evening, alone, was I able to come to terms with the hour in the manager's office. The event was too unexpected. I had trouble believing it had occurred, but the signed documents were irrefutable. Reading them the sanity of his madness was delineated in precise legal language. The facts, sorted through and condensed were simple; I am learning not to look for tricks from this man. I am to receive a yearly allowance of 100,000 pounds sterling to carry on the "project." The definition of the "project" will be worked out by a collaborative effort of the old man and myself in the ensuing month and will be the subject of a future contract. My scepticism was a spent fury.

♦♦♦

She is much more studious and attentive. With the signing of the bank papers she takes me more seriously. Obviously, prior to proof, official documents with signatures under seal, she was merely appeasing my "fantasy," but now, doubt has been replaced by amazed trust.

We have one month in which to describe the course of our project, one more month during which I must stay awake.

The recent news has been dominated by acts of terrorism. An editorial in an obscure news magazine condemns all acts of terrorism, maintaining that the two central purposes of their actions are to force governments to do what they normally won't do, and to obtain media attention for their cause. Exactly, but the editorial makes it appear as though these are the faults and not the strengths of terrorism. A group of hostages, held for seventeen days by a group of Shiite militia who hijacked a TWA Boeing 727, when released had mixed feelings about their captors. Those who were reported as sympathetic to the Shiite cause were being criticized by the

American government in whose view the terrorists were "animals, lunatics who should be hunted down and exterminated." Many of the captives while critical of their captors said they could not help but be sympathetic to their complaints. The media tried to downplay their sympathy by quoting psychologists who analyzed the situation as a common occurrence, a close relationship often develops between captors and captives. The media played up the mixed feelings of the hostages towards their captors. On the negative side was a fifty-seven year-old guide for religious tours who felt: "anger, frustration, a sense of being raped, ravaged by these animals. I think that the President was absolutely right when he called them thugs, thieves and murderers, because that's what they were, thugs." Dr. Toga, an assistant professor of neurology, on his release said: "I have no sympathy for terrorist activities, no matter what the cause." He was justifiably upset, his captors had subjected him to a game of Russian roulette, holding a revolver to his stomach, spinning the cylinder and pulling the trigger. Richard P. Herzgerg, one of the men separated from the other hostages in Lebanon because of his Jewish-sounding name, said the terrorists had "duped the American public into thinking this was fun and these were nice people. The people who took us off the plane are vile, disgusting animals. These are animals and they should be treated as animals. They should be brought to justice somehow."

On the other side many of the hostages urged the American government to meet the Shiite demand, the Israel release of 735 Lebanese prisoners, most of them Shiites.

There was a "profound sympathy for the cause, or for the reasons that the Amal had in saying, 'Israel, free my people.'" During their captivity the hostages ate "good rice and good meat" from "the best restaurant in Beirut." They were learning about Amal's cause, but without brainwashing. "They are living a very rich experience." And there was the farewell dinner party thrown by the captors at a seaside hotel called the Summerland. The hostages and guards, with ABC television present, sat down to a festive dinner of hamburgers, club sandwiches, orange juice and soft drinks. At the end of the meal, the hotel management brought out a large sponge cake decorated with the words: WISHING YOU ALL A HAPPY TRIP HOME. It was a sentimental evening. Some of the hostages exchanged roses with their guards. One American said: "I will be coming back to Lebanon. Hamiye (one of the jailors) is like a brother to me." Another said: "This is a beautiful country — like Miami, in many ways. Amal has tried to tell us what they feel about war, they hate it. They want a better life, just like you and me."

Not one move in this terrorist drama was made without the presence of the media. Everyone was typecast. A seventeen day mini-drama written by the Shiites. I wouldn't leave the room. It brought me strength. She would bring in stockpiles of junk food and we would sit glued to the television consuming corn chips and pizza as the hostages and captors waved to the cameras in "Let's Make a Deal" and "Nabih Berri Knows Best." The networks fought bitterly for the honour of being manipulated most often by the Shiites. The Amal militiamen — producers of the program — auctioned off a session with the hostages, $12,500. The Shiites played favourites, honouring ABC's Charles Glass, a veteran of Middle-eastern coverage, for helping keep the network's bureau open the previous year when most other American news organizations had pulled out. No one helped the print press, well aware of television's superior strength. And we sat watching our favourite characters and tried to predict the next turn of events.

When it was all over the terrorists had obviously won, besides speeding the release of their Shiite comrades they had captured the media, taken their message to the world. When asked: "Did you approve of the hijackings?" Sheik Ibraham al Amin, the leader of Hizbullah, the militant Shiite organization whose militiamen carried out the TWA hijacking, answered:

> I agree that people should be given the right to express their opinion of the injustice inflicted on them. The hijacking should be understood from this point of view. Instead of considering the matter terrorism and enmity to the American people, which they are not, Americans should think about the policy of their government toward the people of the Middle East. The American government is responsible for this action. Why didn't the American people denounce this matter? It is tied to the problem of the detainees in Israel. It is a human-rights issue. The pressure should be directed to releasing all the detainees.

The President: They are barbarians.

Sheik al Amin: For several years America has been sucking the blood of our people.

The President: We have our limits — and our limits here have been reached, this cannot continue.

Sheik al Amin: These people have the willingness to die with pride and dignity and become an example for all freedom seekers in the world. They are not terrorists. We have not gone to America, we haven't bombed the American people. The Americans come to us.

The United States having lost this small skirmish has decided to wage a full scale war against terrorism. Doesn't the US realize that for the past thirty years it has been waging a war encouraging terrorism? What does one do against a large war machine, confront it head on? No, one uses cunning. She looks at me, smiles, I smile back. What do the weak do against the strong, what does the ant do with the mountain? Of course, the US will roar in anger after being stung by the bee. She tosses me a chocolate bar — my taste buds wake for the first time in ten years and the chocolate possesses a sweet pleasure. It's obvious, our project, we both are acting like children throwing food and pillows around the room.

◆◆◆

We have decided on Africa. And then the difficult task of compiling information about every African country. Reading the daily newspapers is almost useless: the most minor local event is given the front page, banner headlines, while news affecting the life-and-death struggle of millions on another continent is omitted entirely. We buy every possible news magazine originating from or dealing specifically with the Third World. We spend our afternoons together trying to understand the current Africa.

His energy fluctuates from energetic exuberance to deep sleep without warning or explicit cause.

Sudan. Here is a country which offers some possibility. The serious state of their economy: burdened by an outstanding debt of $9 billion US; a stagnating domestic sector; and trouble in the country's South. And the President, Gaafar Mohammed Nimeriri, recently announced the introduction of the Sharia — Islamic law — hoping to create an Islamic republic in Sudan, raising the opposition to a frenzy. There is a possibility of a coup by lower ranks in the army. An interesting situation. Volatile. Worth our consideration.

Upper Volta. There has already been a progressive revolution. The new leader is Captain Thomas Sankara, one of West Africa's new generation of young military ideologues, at thirty-four one of the youngest. The new ruling body — the National Council for the Revolution (CNR) — is dominated by civilians. Sankara is purging the military, retiring or putting on trial conservative officers. The CNR has enacted a far-reaching plan to draw the people into politics by creating committees for the Defence of the Revolution (CND's). There are economic and drought problems, but the course of the country is in the right direction. No need here for our intervention.

Each nation is considered in its turn and often as not I find myself speaking to a sleeping man. It doesn't make a difference, when the problem is solved he will be awake.

✦✦✦

Really, it's not worth it. Getting up. No not a chance of success. A hopeless fantasy. What are we going to do together? Nothing. My body doesn't really see the necessity of exerting the extra strength to walk from the bed to the table; it can lay here as well as sit there. I'd rather not, and I can't think of any reason why I should. If there was the possibility of a development rather than history. She tries to tell me there is still a chance, there is a mark yet to be made on history. I am too tired, just my body, it wants to lie down. I don't want to stare at the ceiling. She says if only I will get up, she'll help. But I won't get up; my body doesn't want to any more; nothing either of us says will change its mind; nothing we can do will confuse it from the sheets.

She grabs hold of my arm, by the wrist and shoulder, pulling, stuffing pillows behind my back. She has me sitting. Balancing a tray on my knees — spoonfeeding tea and well-cut corners of dry toast.

How long can a man live on tea and toast?

Removing the tray, spreading an atlas, a map of Africa. Hopefully inspiration. A trick to wake me.

Mauritania

Spanish Sahara

Mali

Senegal

Gambia

I am too tired. Eyes closed. She shakes me once, but it is no good. Merely a distant wind. There are no powerful muscular contractions remaining, no possibility that I will raise the gun to his chest and even if it were not necessary to try three times he would not die at my hand.

◆◆◆

In the half light of the room I watch him sleep. He changes positions frequently, back, side, stomach; this isn't the sleep of rest — when he wakes he will be tired and discouraged. The wrinkles on his face and neck appear deeper during sleep, tightening rather than relaxing.

My mistake has been the attempt to pinpoint one locale for our project. The mode of reasoning embodied in the process of confining action through locale is obsolete, based on armchair praxis. Media has imploded all locales into one common electronic space. My calculation of the map has been a waste of energy. I might as well spin the globe and randomly place my finger, a game. But intuitively, the educated guess of my spinning-globe-system of selection, persists on naming Africa.

It is self evident.

Interviewer: How do you define the responsibility of the outside world to help resolve Africa's food problems?

President of the World Food Council: There is no way we can say we are civilized if we let Africa starve. This is worse than the Holocaust, because we are aware of what is going on and we can stop it if we want to.

We estimate some 34 million people could die from malnutrition, exposure and disease because of the draught and famine in Africa over the next three or four years.

The United States has paid its own farmers $19 billion not to produce wheat and corn. This is economics at its worst and is more than the whole world spent on food aid in any one year.

In international organizations there is too much paper pushing and studying, too much waste and duplication, not enough action. There is not enough concern when we stay in our air conditioned offices. Not enough of us get out into the field for a real understanding of the death and poverty there.

He has recently acquired the disconcerting ability to remain asleep and open his eyes. The first demonstration was three weeks ago, the day of the bank signing, he rolled over in bed onto his side and began staring inquisitively at me. I sat in the armchair trying to piece together the confusing events of the day. I asked him a minor question about the contract but he didn't answer. When I asked him again, slightly louder, I noticed his eyes weren't aimed exactly at me, but rather were focused on the door frame slightly to my right. He was asleep. I wanted to reach over and close his eyes, pushing the eyelids down into their proper position, but I couldn't, this was something one only did with the dead, and to do it would be — I was afraid it would actually occur — to pronounce him dead.

◆◆◆

Media makes history. In the past it may have been actual events, their importance measured in a scale of magnitude, weight of repercussion, but today the measurement is distorted by the media. A minor event given full and extended coverage by the international media becomes loaded with historic importance. A major event unrecorded by the media becomes a nonevent. The more who are informed of an event the greater the possibility of affecting the consciousness of a greater number. At the same time, the media homogenizes all events, turning everything into an ephemeral new item, and this is a major problem: media's voracious appetite demanding a constant flow of new news, the constant demand to turn its attention to a fresh topic. The media is quickly bored, a fickle lover. The first challenge is to capture its gaze, make it turn its monolithic electronic eye in your direction. The second challenge is to compel its attention, holding it is the beginning of history.

Some might complain, this is not history at all, but a transitory sensationalism, how does this compare with the solid history of, for example, the Boer War? But it does, it is our history, the solid ephemerability of a hundred Boer Wars occurring every day, our hundredfold expansion of history. Today not even the reporters watch the battlefield from a nearby hill, we all sit with the generals in our living rooms, the children on the rug.

I have no doubts about any of these observations. Our project must be grounded in an understanding of media. A protest march of 100,000 carrying placards, chanting slogans, holding hands is unnoticed, and ineffective if the media does not expand the local route of their march. One well-planned TV commercial broadcast at prime time is a more effective use of energy, time and money for the 100,000 marchers unless the media deems their cause newsworthy. The media doesn't know the difference between just and unjust causes. Buy time, make commercials and sell your cause.

If you don't have the money to buy media time, stage an event, perpetuate an entertainment spectacle. And here I am dressing, putting on my make-up, testing my movements, the tone of my voice, preparing myself for the herd of reporters, the klieg lights, the cameras and the microphones. I have prepared speeches. The entertainment value of my history has been carefully calculated; the musicians are tuning their instruments; my co-stars are ready. The media is a faithful dog who comes to me fully trained; I can easily predict its response to each of my cues.

◆◆◆

The worst possible terrorism is the terrorism of blood, where the first action is to draw blood, to kill, where there is no possibility to negotiate. These are the acts whose motives arc revenge against a difficult enemy, carried out to remind the enemy there is still active opposition. These are the coward terrorists who act against unarmed civilians. These are the terrorists who live like rats and think like rats. These are the terrorists who live in a psychopathic past without understanding the modern world.

What good does it do to place a bomb on an airplane and kill 329 innocent people, what sympathy is illicited for the cause, who have they educated to their "just complaints"? What have they proved but their ability to kill? The media concerns itself with the victims and condemns the killers. The Indian government hasn't been threatened, pressured or made to evaluate or substantiate its position in public. The worst has occurred, the irrationality of the attack proves that harsh measures must be undertaken, suppression is called justice when it is directed against lunatic murders. No, the terrorism of blood is weakness not strength, stupidity not intelligence. Terrorism can and should be employed from a weak position, but it has to be done with daring, cunning, devoid of revenge, not in the name of blood, but as a just means of manipulating an entrenched enemy. A well-carried out act of terrorism can cut a passage through a mountain, but a foolish act only brings the mountain crashing down on both the innocent and the guilty. The threat of blood and its absence can be a powerful weapon.

Awaken the world's interest, create suspense, force them to wait in their media environments for the drama to unfold, hold them dangling at the edge — balanced — with baited breath. Use the techniques of narrative to your advantage, and then present the happy ending, everyone winning, the absence of victims, the humanity of the protagonist, the sigh of relief, the spontaneous applause. The media will extol your cause to the world and your act will be remembered not for its blood, but its cunning and bravery. The world always wants heroes, and the causes of heroes are always just.

Again our direction is obvious, not even a choice. I tell him and he agrees; he adds the notion that if a tyrant is evil there is nothing wrong with taking their life, blood in this instance being just.

Basically we are agreed. It is becoming clearer and clearer every day. And every day he sleeps more; I become more excited and cannot sleep; the balancing of an equation, the Newtonian notion that energy is never created nor destroyed, merely a transference. I listen to his breathing, it is very light, ethereal, without real substance.

✦✦✦

As much as possible, arrangements have been made. I have my plane ticket and a small bag containing clothing, books and blank paper. Unencumbered with possessions, without ballast. What little clothing I now carry and wear is new, acquired in the last twenty-four hours, some still in their plastic packages. The few books are by authors I have never read. Even the suitcase is new. My present translucent. I am only interested in one tense. When I watch this old man, in bed, sitting, eating, watching television, I am at a distance, already absent, remembering a man who isn't present, a long shadow of the past. I pass him his tea and toast but we hardly converse or exchange looks; I have already departed. It will not be necessary for us to carry on a complex ritual of verbal and gestural farewells.

✦✦✦

I am alone in the room. Arrangements have been made with the hotel management, I will be fed twice daily, although once would have sufficed. The tray is brought by a variety of individuals, no consistency, no cycle, no repetition which I can recognize. I have little desire to sort and match the procession of hands, faces, voices. I have no interest in their food — greasy bacon and eggs, cold boiled potatoes, and over-

185

cooked meat which I couldn't dare begin to chew.

Her departure was without event; from my bed only slightly raising my head from the pillow. To this near stranger, to this passing moment in my life I was entrusting all possibility. Trying to perpetuate, here the attempt, once and once more again.

Bank account numbers and locations throughout the world with signed authority to use the money in any way she may see fit. The Dongo treasure; my share was now hers.

I closed my eyes for a moment. When I woke she was gone.

It had been arranged.

◆◆◆

His bare chest. The chin pressed out for the last time.

Her moment of history will not be an instant, it will be more than one quick burst.

June 28, 1914 the Archduke Ferdinand and his wife Sophie set out in an open car, Sunday, an official visit to Sarajevo, the capital of the Austrian province of Bosnia.

When she discovers the action necessary to achieve our goals we have agreed to act without hesitation. The opportunity must be grabbed quickly. But how long, how many years of nights in our respective rooms will we have to wait?

Among the crowd waiting to greet the Archduke were the

Slav terrorists of the Black Hand Society. She threw a bomb at the royal car, but the crowd was too thick, her arm was hit. Missing. The second car explodes. Two officers are wounded. Some of the crowd shout, it's her, it's her, but she escapes down a narrow street, a back alley, a hidden doorway.

Of all the attempts so many have ended in failure. It is difficult to stand and throw a rock at the advancing army. How many forgotten failures constitute the history which does not exist?

After a speech at the town hall, the Archduke and his wife drive off to visit the seriously wounded officer in the hospital.

To persevere beyond the failure, to lift the gun and when this gun jams, to try a second, and when this gun jams to try a third. In the name of the National Movement of Socialist Democracy, the Temporary Revolutionary Committee, I. Machiavelli said it, the tyrant cannot be left alive or he will return and destroy what you have created... am ordered....

As their royal car passed along the quay beside the river, her friend, her fellow student of revolution, Gavrilo Princip, a man sure of his destiny, his eyes never flinching, fired three shots from a pistol at close range. The Archduke fell, his wife fell. There is no sense in running — they grab him by the shoulders, dragging him by the arms.

These three shots are heard around the world, heard again and again for four years of bloody war.

She promised to telephone; I can hear it ringing. Ringing. They are shaking me by the shoulder. "Will I eat?" Opening my pyjamas, listening to my heart. "Will I eat?" Of course I will, of course I will. It is just a matter of time. Of time. Of course I will.

What will it mean, this empty room? Fresh sheets. Someone will throw a suitcase on the bed, look out the window, try the television and the bath.

And what will they care that my head is still resting on their pillow.

❖❖❖

A haze of images, a drone of sound. The television watches me when I sleep. Someone, soon, will bring food. They are told. Return to sleep? The laughter of a child, a woman's voice, the interior of an orderly household. I'm not in the mood for a domestic scene. Close my eyes. The dramatic music, the stilted dialogue, two lovers lost in the importance of their mutual betrayals. The news. A black youth shot by a policeman in New York. A plane hijacked. Something. I can hear her voice. I lift my head to the television. She is there. Standing next to a hooded man. A gun aimed at her head, pushed against her skin. Held. What is she saying, I can't hear. A demand. And she is gone. Prime Minister Thatcher saying she will not comply with the demands of any terrorist organization. No. She will be here soon. Bringing me a tray of food. I will have tea. She will have coffee. We will share some toast with butter. It has all been carefully arranged. And tomorrow we will go to the restaurant. Yes. Our project. We will talk. Precisely as arranged. A small sleep. Soon she will be here. The softness of the pillow. Someone has turned off the television. Now, if they would only dim the lights. Yes. And tomorrow.

♦♦♦

I have to concentrate, to concentrate. There is no one to ask. To ask when did she leave? How long? Yesterday? This morning? Or is it morning now? I wake from sleep so often. How many times have I awakened since she went? Yesterday? But how many trays of food have been brought? If I can answer these questions I will know, it was her, it wasn't her. I saw, I didn't see, I heard, I didn't hear, on television. And when did I think it was? Another question. It was, for sure, last night. Or this morning. Recently. Since, I have been staying awake, or trying to, waiting for more news. I suspect it hasn't occurred. But it might have.

♦♦♦

I refuse to believe in irony. History may be perverse. But I can't imagine it with a sense of humour.

♦♦♦

A doctor has been called. I ask him if he's heard any news about the hijacking. Have I slept through a broadcast? Has he seen her? Television. He looks at me with bewilderment and asks why I haven't been eating. I'm not interested. I didn't notice. The doctor won't answer my questions. I try to watch the screen but he is standing in the way. I return to sleep. He is forced to depart, a gesture of hope scribbled on a slip of paper, a drug to return my interest in food.

◆◆◆

Yes, I do believe in irony. With a gun at her head. I saw it again. The news. She isn't afraid. She understands the positions of viewing. He won't pull the trigger on camera; not her death he wants. Is it possible, she isn't merely the victim, not the object, but part of the action? Yes, I do believe in irony. Yes, it is possible. Yes. Yes. And alone in his room an old man laughs. The sound of laughter running down the corridors. In a few minutes the bell boys will enter, carefully, thinking it has finally come, everyone heard the old man's death rattle. The humourless don't believe in irony. Only history could have written the scenario.

Printed in Canada